HAG

KATHLEEN
KAUFMAN

HAG

A NOVEL

TURNER PUBLISHING COMPANY

Turner Publishing Company
Nashville, Tennessee
New York, New York
www.turnerpublishing.com

Hag

Cover design: Maddie Cothren
Book design: Meg Reid
Lyric Credit: Kate Rusby, "Planets"

Library of Congress Cataloging-in-Publication Data
Names: Kaufman, Kathleen, author.
Title: Hag : a novel / Kathleen Kaufman.
Description: Nashville, Tennessee : Turner Publishing Company, [2018] |
Summary: Spanning centuries of human history, the daughters of the lowland hag, the Cailleach, an ancient female force hidden in the rocky Scottish cliffs, must navigate a world filled with superstition, hatred, violence, pestilence, and death to find their purpose.
Identifiers: LCCN 2018008658| ISBN 9781684421671 (pbk.)
ISBN 9781684421688 (hard cover)
Subjects: | CYAC: Mythology, Celtic--Fiction.
Classification: LCC PZ7.1.K377 Hag 2018 | DDC [Fic]--dc23
LC record available at https://lccn.loc.gov/2018008658

9781684421671 (PBK)
9781684421688 (HC)
9781684421695 (eBook)

Printed in the United States of America
18 19 20 10 9 8 7 6 5 4 3 2 1

To my mother, who told me all the stories and taught me from a very young age that magic can be found in even the most ordinary of places.

"She is powerful if different."
—Tina Turner

"I have recognized that the All is being dissolved, both the earthly things and the heavenly."
—*Gospel of Mary 8:17*

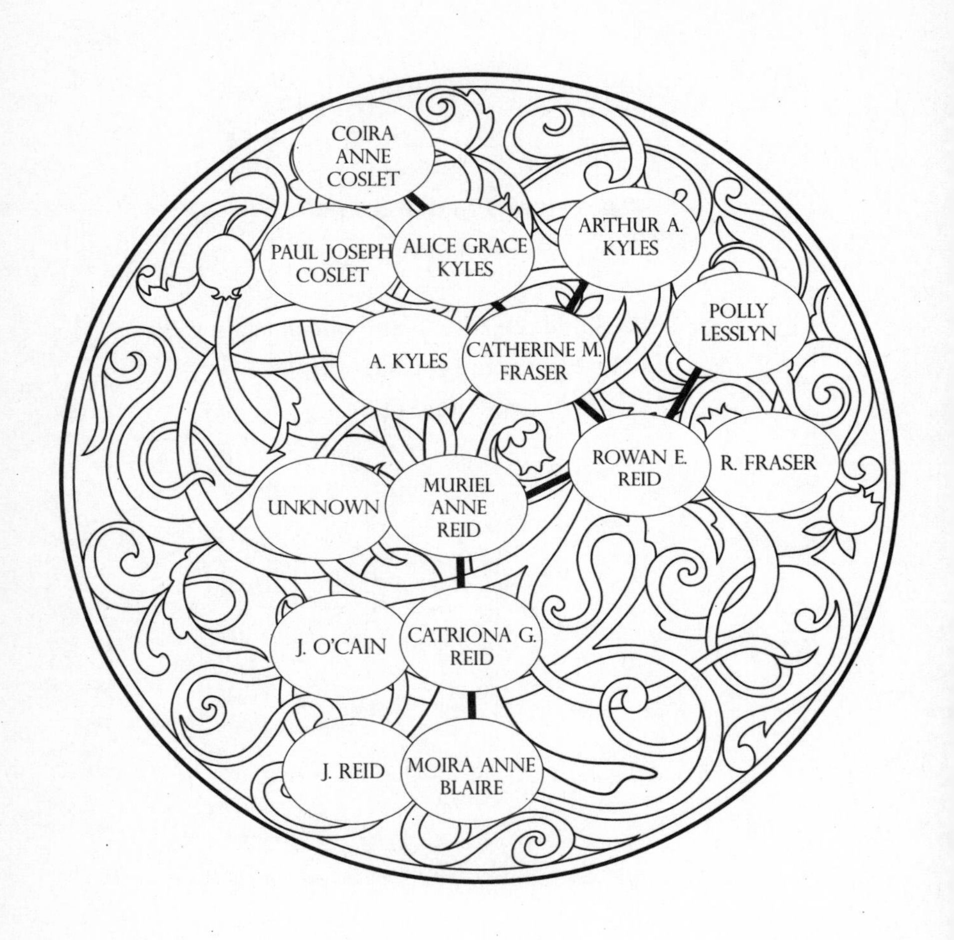
COIRA ANNE COSLET
PAUL JOSEPH COSLET
ALICE GRACE KYLES
ARTHUR A. KYLES
POLLY LESSLYN
A. KYLES
CATHERINE M. FRASER
ROWAN E. REID
R. FRASER
UNKNOWN
MURIEL ANNE REID
J. O'CAIN
CATRIONA G. REID
J. REID
MOIRA ANNE BLAIRE

PROLOGUE

THE LOST VILLAGE STILL STANDS *somewhere deep in the lowland hills. The Cailleach's curse has not waned or weakened. An invisible shield, as permeable as water, surrounds the tiny village surrounded by the rough field grass, not far from the cave where if one looks closely enough, one can still make out the mark of Ingwaz carved on the stones that block the entrance. Over the years, the village has become harder and harder to see; as memory of the Cailleach faded and the raven-haired hag turned to folklore and the folklore became a relic of an ancient time, people forgot, and in their forgetting, they lost the ability to see. Unconsciously and quite by accident, they crossed the Lethe, and their memories of an earlier time when magic was part of the ordinary was erased.*

Now the field is home to a development of flats, parking lots, cars, and paved roads. The rough grass that the daughter of Cailleach ran through in her terror and grief so very many years ago has been cultivated, and rows of manufactured flowers and shrubs fall in neat rows. Children play on a brightly painted climbing frame and laugh as they push each other on the roundabout. They have no memory of those who lived on the land so many years ago. Families sit in their gardens at twilight and hear only the thrush sing out the day.

There is a stretch of land that has never been developed; it sits pristine and untouched, and those who live in this oblivious and forgetful world avoid it entirely. It was deemed unsuitable for structures many years ago, and no one has bothered to examine the diagnosis. A deep and unsettling feeling comes over anyone who lingers in this no-man's-land surrounded by progress. Dogs, run away from their owners, will stop and bark at an invisible enemy on the border of the green space. The children dare each other to walk through the field at night, and every so often a story rises of a single light emanating from the center of the field: as small as a candle flame, it flickers back and forth in the night and then disappears entirely.

CHAPTER 1

BRIGHT RED RAIN BOOTS, boots that were seeing their first good Glasgow rain. Alice Grace is six years old today, and she is wearing brand-new red rain boots from the United States. They arrived via parcel post the week before, and it had been the single most exciting event of the entire dreary week. There was a note enclosed that read, "It rains buckets in the summer, getting you ready for a good Colorado downpour." Her mother had cursed and not apologized. Another thing to pack, why not keep them till we get settled? Alice Grace didn't care a bit about that. She had new red boots and it was raining on High Street, the water winding its way through the cobblestones, creating paths around the broken stone and rubble. She figured in Colorado, United States, the streets were all smooth pavement, the piles of brick and stone, the destruction of the war, were made into clean, straight walls, and the weather was always agreeable. The trees were green year-round, and the damp never hung in the air. She skipped in the gutter where the puddles were deepest and made the biggest splash. The hem of her pink-and-grey dress was damp with the muddy water, but she didn't care a bit about that. Her new red rain boots were magnificent and all was well.

She skipped along the path, her eyes on the autumn sky. It was growing dark and the sun had settled into a slow burn behind the rooftops. There was a sense of everything she would leave behind, and Alice Grace almost lost her broad grin at the thought. She knew, after these short weeks, that her life would change forever and wasn't entirely sure that was a good idea. Mum said there were paths we follow in life, and they decided everything. Alice Grace sometimes wondered if the path here on High Street in Glasgow was the one she would be happiest on. She would grow to run the shop that Mum had run before the war. She would sell herbal tinctures and creams made from the garden that had once bloomed in the back courtyard. She would marry the butcher's son, the boy with the chipped tooth and floppy hair who opened doors for her and gave her a chocolate on Christmas. Even at six, Alice Grace saw the path stretched out in front of her. It was a fine life; they lived over the shop in the flat that had sat empty since the Clydebank Blitz. Their children had floppy hair and Alice Grace's honey-brown eyes. They were happy.

Alice Grace saw other things too: even at six she knew better than to tell anyone what she saw. She saw the butcher's boy double over with a pain in his chest, his hair just beginning to grey. She saw her own honey-eyed children with tears in their eyes. She saw herself dressed in black, her own raven hair streaked with white. She saw the neighbors sitting in their humble den, pints and bottles of whiskey aplenty, the children well asleep or at least pretending. She saw herself running the business alone, a respected businesswoman, content, quiet, and happy. Even at six years old, Alice Grace saw a vision of herself sitting by a fire, a book in her hand and a lady's glass of whiskey on the end table. Her honey-eyed children long ago set out upon their fortunes. She saw herself happy and alone and wondered if she should stay, if this were the best she could do in this life.

The problem was the red rain boots. Living above the shop with the floppy-haired butcher's boy was a choice, but there was no room for bright red rain boots. She was to leave for Colorado, United States, in two weeks' time, and there was adventure to be found. She was sure she would see the paths unfold in time, as they formed; she always had before. The water was pooling in a broad swirl at the crook in the lane. Alice Grace skipped in the shadow of the street and sidewalk, enjoying the spray that showered her in muddy rainwater.

Just as she reached the magnificent, broad lake of muddy water, Alice Grace felt the bottom drop out: her right foot, instead of hitting the hard pavement, kept falling, down and down, down forever. In that moment, as she felt her entire six-year-old self lurch forward and down, she saw another path, one that had lain hidden beneath the muddy water. This one carried her down, down, and she saw her mother, face covered in a black veil and the familiar pints here and there; the butcher's boy, his face red and swollen with tears, sat in a corner. There was no Colorado, United States, in this path, not for her or anyone. This was the end of so many things, and Alice Grace understood in that frozen moment that the devil was many things, and all the things that Mum had ever told her flooded her heart. Be strong and proud, Mum had said as she brushed Alice Grace's raven hair that was touched with fire. She felt Mum's lips on the top of her head and smelled nutmeg and vanilla.

She closed her eyes and, resigned to the fall through the mud that seemed never to end, she was already up to her waist, and the cold rush of the rainwater felt like knives in her skin. She felt a scream tear from her mouth, her voice moving of its own accord. Suddenly, a force she couldn't explain gripped her red rain boot and shoved upward. She felt a pair of strong hands, but that was impossible; her foot was deep in the water and no one was there to catch her, yet still the hands tightened and shoved upward. She swore she heard a grunt of effort in her right ear, and a final heave shoved her back up through the swiftly swirling water, too dark to see a bottom, and back onto the cobblestone street. The impact knocked the wind from her chest, and she lay heaving for breath. Her entire body, now soaked with the mud that had moments before been a delight, was shaking with cold. In her right ear, a hot rush of breath, and the same voice that had grunted before whispered low words that Alice Grace knew immediately were only meant for her. "Mind the break, young one."

The deep voice was replaced with a pitched scream in her left ear, one that was meant not just for her but the entirety of Glasgow, it seemed. Alice Grace turned her head to see Miss Kinnear, the elderly woman who lived two doors down and gave her sweet ginger cookies when the holidays were near. Her face was contorted with something Alice Grace recognized immediately as fear. Other voices joined in as Alice Grace tried to sit up, but every bone in her body felt as though it had been shoved roughly into a sack, taken back out again, and shaken into place.

"She fell straight through, thought she was drowned for sure!" Miss Kinnear wailed. A man that Alice Grace recognized from the Saturday vegetable market on Bell Street was dipping a fallen tree branch into the swirling muddy water.

"Grate broke!" he yelled back, his face paler than Alice Grace remembered. "The water's running straight down, she'd been lost in a minute down there!" All around her doors were opening and faces appearing, and hands on her back and arms pulled Alice Grace to her feet. She shook with cold and shock and was suddenly and rather frighteningly hit with an embrace that nearly knocked her off her already unsteady feet. The smell of nutmeg and vanilla gave Alice Grace leeway to dissolve into the hug as her mother frantically asked the growing crowd what had happened.

"Damnedest thing, really." Miss Kinnear was retelling now with the air of a storyteller who has stumbled on the tale of a lifetime. "I saw the child playing in the water and then down she went, and I thought she was drowned for sure, her head was near clear under in a blink, but then up she came, shooting back up like a fountain. Damnedest thing."

Alice Grace turned her head to watch the man from the Saturday market and several others laying planks of wood from someone's courtyard over the rushing water. As the planks interrupted the flow of the mud, she could see the gaping hole in the lane, the metal grate having been ripped from its place.

"Must've been the angels, it was," Miss Kinnear was now spouting to anyone who'd stayed to listen.

"Nonsense," another said, a woman near her mother's age, who had twin boys whose noses were always sticky with green snot. "The water pushed her out, like a wave on the ocean. The angels, my foot."

Alice Grace's mother, the shock of the moment gone, had quite regained her senses. She pushed Alice Grace back a step and regarded her closely.

"If I ever catch you messin' about in the muck like this again, young lady, you better wish you'd fallen straight through to hell itself, as it would be better than what I'll do to ya!" Her voice rang through the streets, and Alice Grace felt her face growing red. The neighbors shuffled back into their doorways, the drama of a naughty child and a high-handed threat far too ordinary for an audience. Alice Grace's mother nodded a thank-you to the men who continued to barricade the broken grate, and they started back up the lane. The red rain boots were now filled with filthy water and not fun at all. The deep voice in Alice Grace's ear echoed silently, a hymn. As she sat on the front steps of the shop and emptied out her boots, Alice Grace saw another path unfold in front of her, and she said a silent farewell to the butcher's boy and the Glasgow rain.

BACK IN THE DAYS *when time ran sideways and backward and all manner of directions, there was a lowland village that had sat abandoned ever since anyone could remember. The local children would dare each other, in the way that children do, to creep right up to the edge where the knobby field grass met the dirt path. The bravest of the lot could see that the shops and cottages still stood, as though the residents were merely waiting around the corner. The paint never faded, the wood never turned to rot, flowers grew in neat paths along the walkway, and a very small boy with dishwater-dull hair had even claimed to have seen a candle burning in a window.*

Hogwash was what the women and men in the surrounding lowland hills said. Everyone knew that the cholera had taken the village, and the stink of infection still lay over it, and it was a fool's game to get too close.

There's a terrible expanse between childhood and adulthood. The children would have been well-advised to stay away from the lost village, and the grown ones would be well-advised to believe in things more evil than the cholera. As it was, both groups stuck to their version of the truth and none was the wiser for it.

CHAPTER 3

ALICE IS EIGHT YEARS old today. She is no longer Alice Grace, as she's discovered that real Americans didn't use both their names, so in addition to doing everything possible to cover her Glasgow accent, she dropped her second name. Mum had rolled her eyes and not commented when Alice informed her in clipped American speech that she was no longer Alice Grace, just Alice. The two years since their arrival in Colorado, United States, had been somewhat uneventful. The house on Twenty-First Street, Colorado Springs, had a large front porch with a rail that ran clear around the sides. Alice liked to sit on it and dangle her legs, watching the cars drive past. There had been cars in Glasgow, of course, but not nearly so many, nor so many different sorts. Her family did not have a car. Mum said it was a luxury they surely didn't need. Alice thought it would be nice not to have to walk the groceries back from the market every Saturday or wheel the laundry in the squeaky-jointed cart every Sunday afternoon. The school bus picked her up on the next block; but even at that, the winter wind in Colorado, United States, wasn't any kinder than it had been in Glasgow. But it was autumn now and not time for the winter wind. It was Alice's favorite time of year, and not just because of her birthday. It was time for sweaters, hand-knitted by Aunt Polly. Mother didn't knit sweaters, but she did sew little patchwork bears and tigers from squares of old clothes. She gave the lot of them to the church for the poor children, but when she caught Alice looking at one in particular, it usually made its way to her bed and joined the growing tribe of animals that resided there.

Alice could smell her birthday cake baking. Aunt Polly had made it from scratch, as she did for everyone's birthdays. Her brother, Arthur, had spent the morning dancing around the kitchen begging for a spoon to lick or a dab of stray icing. A year ago, Alice would've raised hell; it was her birthday, after all, and any spoons that needed licking should be licked by her and her alone. But she was eight today and too mature for such carrying on. Arthur was five and still a baby. He could fuss over the cake icing as much as he liked. This made Alice feel both incredibly grown-up and sad at the same time.

"Alice!" Her mother called from the kitchen. "Alice, we're short of eggs; you need to run to the corner market if you want meringue."

Alice grinned. It was widely known in her house that meringue was supposed to be intended for pie only, but Alice had always insisted it was wasted on such a limited path. She had begged Aunt Polly to make a cake with the fluffy sugar topping. Mother and Aunt Polly had laughed and sent her outside, but this errand meant she had won. Her mother appeared at the door, a smile on her face, making her look years younger. She handed Alice a couple of dollar bills and a handful of quarters. "Get some milk too while you're there. And hurry, and watch the cars." She paused before closing the door and leaned over to land a kiss on Alice's head. "Crazy girl, meringue on cake." She shook her head as she re-entered the house, but she was still smiling. Alice smiled back even though Mum couldn't see.

It was a perfect day. The leaves were a combination of red and gold and they crunched under Alice's feet. The sky was a perfect, cloudless blue with just the right amount of bite to the air. Alice looked at the pile of money in her hand. Her mother had given her enough for eggs, milk, and even a sweet. Alice carefully placed the bills and coins in the pocket of her jumper and set off down the sidewalk. The corner market was only a block away, but it was a welcome adventure. Mother worried about the cars; she worried Alice and Arthur would wander into the street without looking. She worried that the cars themselves would jump right up onto the sidewalk and run them down. She worried that the cars would burst straight into flames as they drove and Alice would be caught in the chaos. Alice didn't know much about how cars worked, but she was pretty sure the sidewalk-and-fire bit was something of a worthless worry. As for the street, she was always careful, more so when Arthur walked with her—as they did every morning for school.

Alice had been right about the sweet. She bought a penny licorice and walked slowly back, the grocery sack under her arm. She played a game where she tried to step on as many leaves as possible. An older woman who reminded her of Miss Kinnear from the lane in Glasgow waved at her from her front porch. The house was painted a frosty pink and reminded Alice of a fluffy cake. The old woman called Alice "Scottish Girl" and liked to pinch her cheeks. Alice was rather glad she was too far away to do it now; the day had been perfect so far and that would have been an unwelcome interruption. She waved back and kept to the course of crushing each red-and-gold leaf under her new Mary Jane school shoes. She was nearly at the corner, where it would be time to pay more attention and stop playing, when she heard the screech of tires and a long, thin scream that made Alice drop both the remaining licorice and the grocery bag. In front of her, a child with a wool cap and matching vest was lying in a growing pool of blood. A bicycle lay twisted in a nearly unrecognizable puzzle a few yards away. A farmer's truck, older than any of the cars she usually saw in this neighborhood, was turned sideways, blocking the street. An old man lay slumped over the steering wheel, blood leaking from his bald head onto the rusted paint of the truck.

Alice screamed and stared at the scene. She didn't know what to do, and the boy was dead; she knew it to be so. Her legs were frozen to the spot, and she didn't know what the right thing to do was. The boy was dead, and in that moment she saw his whole path as it had been laid out. He was on his way with the daily papers; his job was to throw them onto the porches and steps of all the houses. He was to go home straight after and give his father the money he earned that day straight away. Alice imagined that the boy would do this for many years, and one day he would leave. He would take a train to a city far away that Alice didn't know, but the towers shot into the sky, and as many cars as she saw here, there were a million more there. The boy wanted to write stories, and he would be successful after a time. His stories would be handed to all the schoolchildren and they would be made to read them. He was to die an old man, alone but happy, surrounded by the things that had given him comfort in his life: an old pipe that had belonged to his father, a stack of books with notes upon notes written in the sides, a pillow his mother had sewn for him as a child, a hand-stitched train as the border. He had an equally old cat who lay on his chest in the end. Alice could feel the grumbling purr fill the man's chest, and he was glad for his life.

But that would never happen now. The boy lay in the street, blood already starting to clot in places and his skin taking on a greyish tint. Alice screamed and felt her stomach drop out from under her. When she opened her eyes, the woman from the fluffy pink cake house was looming over her. Others were there too, drawn from their houses by the commotion.

"Scottish Girl!" the old woman snapped. "What's all this about? Are you hurt?" She looked around at the others. "Heard her carrying on, and then she just passed clean out. Probably gave herself a good goose egg on the back of her head."

Alice looked around wildly. Why were they all staring at her? The boy was dead, the old man in the truck—why wasn't anyone helping them? She sat up, feeling the blood rush to her head, nearly making her faint again. "The boy! He's dead! I know he is! The truck, he was hit on his bicycle! I saw it all!"

"Hush, child." The old woman said a bit more gently than before. "There's nothing. You must have thought you saw something, but look, child, there's nothing."

Alice looked at the street where the blood and twisted metal had just been. It was empty of cars or boys. Red and gold leaves swirled in the breeze. The neighbors who had come out to look slowly returned to their houses. The old woman helped Alice to her feet and handed her the grocery bag.

"Oh, look there, you've gone and smashed all your eggs. Your mother will have your head. Come with me, I'll give you a few of mine. Better than going home empty-handed." With that, the old woman took Alice's hand and pulled her back down the sidewalk to the fluffy pink cake house.

Afterward, Alice walked more somberly, a half dozen of the old woman's eggs in her grocery bag. She played out what she had seen. It was so real, but it couldn't have been, could it? The boy was still on that corner, and every act was a reminder of what was supposed to happen. Alice didn't understand why what was supposed to happen wasn't what really happened, or how she knew the difference.

Later that evening, the meringue cake eaten and a new pair of woolen socks and matching sweater unwrapped, she lay in her bed. She wondered where the boy was now. She hadn't spoken of the incident to Mum or Aunt Polly. She had hugged Arthur extra hard before he went to bed, and Mum had looked at her oddly but not commented on it. Where did you go when your path was interrupted? Were you destined to play out the error for all eternity? At church, they spoke of the eternity of the spirit. Alice shivered with horror at the thought of reliving such an ill-gotten death for all time.

CHAPTER 4

THE LOST VILLAGE MIGHT *have slipped from view altogether had it not been for a very small boy with dishwater-dull hair. On the solstice night, when the grown ones were toasting the turning of the season and the night was as long as it ever would be, the little boy took off toward the lost village on a dare. The other boys had mocked him; he hadn't seen a candle, they all said, he was a liar and he made up stories. The little boy, in a mixture of bravery and stifled tears, had stared them all down and set off in the summer twilight. The other boys hooted and called and eventually followed. A peeping courage overtaking them, they followed the wee boy through the brush and across the prickly field grass, all the way to the dirt path that led into the village. Once there they held back, watching and waiting with their torments and insults. He hadn't seen anything, they cried after him; he was a baby, they jeered, as the little boy with the dishwater-dull hair continued on, determined to prove them wrong.*

But the very little boy with the dishwater hair didn't stop at the path on that solstice night. The little boy stepped onto the walkway and marched into town on shaking legs. He looked back as he entered the arch that signaled the start of the main stretch of what had been shops and merchants. The boys would later say he said a word to them, or maybe a phrase. But the wind had picked up and they couldn't hear. In their memory he mouthed a name, but not any name they knew—a curse.

Cailleach.

It hadn't made sense, but when they told the grown ones back home in a fit of panic and fear, the grown ones' faces had turned pale. That was the end of the game, until, of course, it began again as memories faded.

CHAPTER 5

ALICE IS IN QUITE a lot of trouble. The new flannel pajamas that Mum gave her for Christmas are not in the drawer where she had placed them so carefully just a few hours earlier. She received two presents that year: a small glass jar of bath beads that smelled like vanilla and honey, and the red-and-green flannel pajamas. She knew Mum was in no position to give her anything that year and hadn't expected the gift, but there it had been anyhow, wrapped in cheerful green tissue paper with curling ribbons falling off the side. Alice had squealed and hugged them to her chest.

The winter nights were cold and the new house was drafty. Mum said it would get better as they worked on the nooks and crannies, but for now the wind whistled in through the window frames and under the crooked doors. Alice and Arthur had one room, Mum another, and Aunt Polly the third. There was a long kitchen with two counters and electric plugs and a brand-new electric stove. A dark wood table flanked the kitchen, big enough for everyone to sit at and look out over the never-ending woods that served as a backyard. If you hiked far enough back, there was a valley where wild raspberry bushes grew. Mum said Alice was liable to get eaten alive by the bears if she insisted on going back there alone. Alice wasn't worried, though; bears were skittish creatures, and she made sure not to linger when she saw their prints.

Mum and Aunt Polly talked about getting a television set, and Alice thought it would be marvelously exciting. So far, though, they were stuck with the radio, but at the local library sale Mum had acquired a set of tapes of a radio show about the Shadow. "Only the Shadow knows," it would start, and Alice would giggle madly and pull Arthur closer when he hid his eyes.

At night, they would sit on the back porch with its sturdy pine rail and look up at the stars. Alice wondered if there were a bigger place on the entire earth than this, and certainly none as lucky. At times, she would feel herself lost in the million specks of light, her soul spread out among the night sky. A bit away in the woods, a neighbor man with an accent that reminded Alice of Glasgow had rolled a sizeable boulder and two tree stumps together, forming a tea table of sorts. Alice had laughed when she saw it and spent many afternoons sitting on the smooth tree stump, her favorite stuffed bear, Angus, sitting across from her. She was too old for such nonsense, she knew, soon to be a teenager, but here in the shade of the pine trees no one could see and no one cared.

She could hear Mum playing the piano from the tree-trunk tea table. Mum tutored the neighborhood children and was planting a garden like the one she had had in Glasgow. The idea was that she could make her lotions and oils and sell them the same way she'd done back in Scotland. Aunt Polly taught the children at the primary school and kept the books at the church.

Alice kept careful track of such things. This house was a marvel, a shell of a cabin when Mum and Aunt Polly had bought it. It had sat empty for so long that it was in dire need of repairs, but a crew of men from the neighborhood were soon sawing and hammering away, and eventually the cracks in the walls were sealed and the floor was smooth and even. Alice and Arthur's room had two small windows and room for two twin beds. Alice understood what this meant to her Mum and aunt. It was a place that no one could ever take from them. There was no landlord, no one to turn them out or tell them they couldn't have a dog. It was a chance to rebuild what they had left behind in Glasgow. Although she and Arthur were, of course, left out of this discussion, Alice understood that it had taken everything they had to buy this bit of land in the mountains outside Colorado Springs, nestled at the base of Pike's Peak. The house was a work in progress; for a time, the water hadn't been running properly, so she and Arthur had been responsible for dragging up buckets of water from the well at the base of the hill out back so the toilet would flush properly. That issue fixed, the electric power continued to be problematic, and they frequently sat in the light of lanterns and candles and ate cold beef and apples for dinner.

Everything considered, Alice had not expected to receive the pajamas, and now they were gone. She knew exactly where she had put them, and it was no use to question Arthur: he was long asleep, his face pale and his breathing raspy. Mum had been too worried about him to ask Alice why she was wearing her old tattered nightdress. Alice lay still in her bed, listening to his wheezing breath. She could see his path and pushed it back, back, back to the bottom-most part of her head. Knowing things was terrible. Instead, she closed her eyes and tried to hear the spirits.

It didn't take too terribly long before she heard soft giggling in the hallway and a conversation just out of range to articulate the words. Alice winced as footsteps ran up and down the hall, knuckles rapping the wall as it went, the sound so loud she was sure it would wake up the entire house. It never did, though; she seemed to be the only one who could hear such things. Mum told her the spirits chose with whom they wanted to speak, and she shouldn't trust everything they said. Alice knew that well enough, but they rarely ever spoke to her directly: most of the time they danced in and out of the sides of her vision, reminding her of things and moving odds and ends around.

Usually it was harmless, like the time Mum's car keys had ended up in the shower stall back in Aunt Polly's tiny bathroom. The adults had all shot fire at Alice and Arthur over the missing keys, and Arthur had cried. But Alice knew better. It wasn't they who moved things around, and Arthur wasn't quite so good at not caring if he got blamed.

The pajamas were a legitimate problem, though; car keys were one thing, but her brand-new Christmas pajamas were another. Mum had spent the sum of two weeks' science tutoring on them. Alice knew because she had heard her and Aunt Polly talking at the kitchen table when they thought everyone was asleep. Mum felt guilty that Alice had taken on so much, especially with Arthur. He needed his medicine at certain times, and it was Alice's job to make sure that he took it and then had a good nap. He needed to eat a bit when he woke up, and Alice took care that he had a bit of toast or an apple if there were any to have. Alice wouldn't allow herself to look too closely at his path, even though it glowed bright as the stars at night. Some things don't need to be acknowledged to be true.

CHAPTER 6

THERE'S A PRICE FOR *the seeing: that was what the grown ones told the boys. It was an expression that meant nothing and eventually made a strange sort of sense. They had long forgotten about the wee boy with the dishwater-dull hair, who would be a grown one himself by now. No one remembered the boy, and if they did, they did not speak of it. A nightmare was all it was. But all the same, those who had a memory to lose warned the children against exploring so far from home. Nothing good will come of it, and for a time the children believed them. The stink of disease and death hung over the countryside. No one spoke of the towns, stricken by cholera or the plague, that had crumbled to the ground from neglect, the stone houses chipping away from disuse, the wood rotting in the damp. No one spoke of the little village, deep on the end of the lowland heath that stood untouched and utterly alone.*

At night, they whispered stories to the children about the Cailleach who lived in the crags and rocks. When the winds whipped the sea to the shore and the rain fell so hard that it was liable to knock a man off his feet, they muttered about the storm hag and left tiny dishes of salt on the window frames. When it came time to harvest the fall crops, the children giggled at the rough corn dollies made from sheaves of grain and left in the field at the end of the last day of the fall harvest. The grown ones shuddered to be the last finished, as that unfortunate soul took on the care of the Cailleach for the winter. It would be their duty to leave a bit of grain or salt, a bit of broth or dried meat. They would move the carved rune stones away from the entrance to the cave overlooking the glen and move them back into place on the first day of summer. They would not forget, or else the crops would die and spring lambs would be stillborn. Children would wander into the mist and get lost among the wood folk; newborns would shrivel and die in their mother's arms. So while the children laughed and played at twisting the rough stalks of grain into grotesque figures, the grown ones watched the sun's position in the sky and hoped they were not the last one left in the field.

CHAPTER 7

ALICE IS GETTING MARRIED. What had started as a punch line to an argument had turned into a call to the community chapel to see about open dates and an appointment with the woman down the street who made the flower arrangements for the baptisms and funerals. Alice felt her whole body turning steadily to ice with each plan made and each phone call placed. Mum stormed about the house as though the very walls were to blame. Aunt Polly had a bottle of whiskey hidden in her room, which made it one of many she'd had in the past year. She'd met a man a bit over a year ago, and there had been talk of a wedding, but just before they were to start the planning and the flowers and all the whatnot, he'd run off with a woman he'd met in town. The woman was fifteen years younger than Aunt Polly and most certainly a whore to hear Mum and Aunt Polly talk.

"They'll have to wear pink; it's all we have. The old choir dresses can be mended but I don't have time to dye them, so pink it will be," Mum said into the phone, arranging the flower girls who would serve in Alice's soon-to-be ill-gotten wedding.

"Fine then, looks like we have the chapel for a week from Sunday. Yes, right after the service, no need to make everyone come back. We'll arrange a potluck, it'll save us the trouble of sending invitations out, don't know who'd come anyhow." Mum cast Alice a spiteful look as she said the last bit.

The whole thing had started a week before, when Alice had been caught kissing a handsome but dim-witted blond boy behind the baseball diamond at the high school. The school principal had dragged her to the office and called Mum, who had driven surprisingly fast and picked her up. Far into the argument about what everyone would think of her, Alice had declared that it didn't matter, she and the boy were getting married, they loved each other and no one could say otherwise. It wasn't entirely a lie, he had proposed to her; however, Alice had laughed him off. They were still in school, and besides, this wasn't her path, and while he was handsome, he was exceedingly dumb. As Aunt Polly was prone to say: "sharp as a bag of hammers." Which in itself didn't make much sense, as hammers did, indeed, have sharp bits, but Alice understood the futility of questioning idioms.

Alice had had to call the poor boy, her voice shaking and her tears threatening to tear her throat clear open, and tell him that yes, indeed, she would marry him. He was very quiet for a moment, and Alice understood very suddenly that he had not been all too serious about it either. But now it was very serious, and his mother and Mum had planned nearly every detail. The handsome yet dull-witted young man was set to graduate in the spring, and his plump mother said Alice could live with them while her son attended the trade school and studied carpentry and electrics so he could pass the union test like his father, who in addition to being a bit simple was also exceedingly portly. Seeing the two of them standing next to each other had given Alice a glimpse at the boy's future. Once the young man joined the union, they could move into a small apartment in town, and his mother would be happy to watch the children as soon as they arrived, which presumably would be soon.

They had a path all lined up, but it wasn't the path that Alice had seen so many years before on the cobblestone lane back in Glasgow. It was enough to give her pause, though; perhaps it would be a happier road. Knowing what lay ahead made an apartment with the boy not look as terrible as it really was. It wasn't any use, though; Alice knew this wouldn't work out, something would break it soon enough, no matter how her Mum and the others chattered about it, and no matter how many choirgirl dresses they hemmed and flowers they ordered. The stars had no intention of letting this path unfold. Alice was almost curious as to what would happen to break up the ever-solidifying plans.

Later that night, as she lay in her twin-sized bed, she looked across the room to the far window. If she lay silent, she could almost hear Arthur breathing. It was a lie, she knew. He wasn't here and hadn't been for some time. She'd hoped his spirit would stay on, talk to her, let her know what to expect next, run down the hall and rap his knuckles on the walls like the spirits that still kept her up at night. But Arthur had left in a single breath, his frail body shuddering one last time and going still. Alice had sat with him for a long while before alerting Mum and Aunt Polly. She knew there was no reason to rush him to the hospital; she had seen this moment from the time he was born and loved him more for it. She knew from the time she first held him in her arms that he wasn't long for this life, and that she must love him enough to make his visit to this world worth the pain it brought. He had looked at her with his great honey-brown eyes, his face pale and scared. He had tried to whisper to her, but his voice was gone, so she had to read his lips. Thank you, he had said. Thank you. He'd never been able to run a block, he'd never know what it was to fall in love, and he'd never dance with Alice at her wedding or play in the ocean. He would never know a world outside of this house, and he had said thank you. Alice shook with the grief that still haunted her years later.

No one had been the same, as was predictable. The living room and long kitchen table had been full of well-wishers and glasses of whiskey. Alice had hidden in their shared room until it was all over. The chaplain, who used to be a rabbi back in his country but had had to flee with his family, had knocked gently and entered the room. He sat on Arthur's ruffled bed, and his face looked so sad that it broke Alice's heart to see it.

"I've lost many people in my life, my own mother and father were lost in the war, in the camps." He looked at Alice for a long moment then, and she saw the horror that he spoke of, a path in reverse, grainy as they were when she saw things already past. She felt her chest unhinging.

"I don't tell you to add to the sadness, child; it's only that one who has seen death knows better than most the pain it causes." He spoke quietly, resigned and weary. Alice nodded quietly.

"It doesn't do much good to talk of God's plan and whatnot. Paths collide and accidents happen, tragedy is senseless, but that doesn't make it easier. You have to keep breathing child, and every day a new sun rises." He rose and paused in the doorway, one last look, and he left.

Alice lay on her bed, missing Arthur and replaying the rabbi's words from years ago in her head while her terrible wedding was being planned outside the door. Easier though it was, she was not meant to live in an apartment with a union man, her children would not be watched by his enthusiastic mother, and there was no cause for the two of them to keep hemming the pink choirgirl dresses. With a deep breath, she left the room to end the charade; she was calling off the whole thing. This had been a game of chicken, and she was declaring herself the loser. Mum's steel will had proved stronger than hers. Alice had blinked first and would call the sweet, stupid boy and tell him the wedding was cancelled. She suspected he would be quietly relieved. His mother would cry and storm about and forget soon enough. Mum would say nothing at all, and with a raise of her eyebrows, she would set to calling the woman down the street and cancelling the flowers. For her part, Alice would go back to her twin bed in her empty room and whisper the story to Arthur, just in case he was still listening.

CHAPTER 8

EVERY PASSING GENERATION *or so, the Cailleach took a man to be her mate and live with her in the highland crags. He would father a child, and together they would live by the still, black waters of the underground lake that lay deep below the lowland heath, set deep within the enchanted caves. They lived there together in this forgotten and quiet place until he died of old age or she tired of his company and set him back on the road, his memory of the time he'd spent in the cave a blind spot in his vision. The Cailleach suffered neither from time nor the elements and outlived all her mates. Her daughters—they were always daughters—grew up a confusing mixture of magical and ordinary. Half hag and half flesh-and-blood. They left when they became women and quickly forgot where they came from, as was the way with enchantment. They married and had daughters and sons of their own and told vague stories of their childhoods, so much forgotten and lost that anyone who listened figured they had seen a horror so great that they had willfully forgotten the past.*

It was quite the opposite: the Cailleach was a loving and generous mother; she shared the secrets of the earth and trees, taught them the birdsong and how to move the clouds and bring the rain. She taught them how to keep the soil fertile and a lullaby to sing to the newly born when they suffered from the grippe. She taught them the words to whisper to the night breeze that would bring a departed soul to the next world. She taught her daughters how to see into the past and the future and how time is running in all directions all the time. She taught them that all the paths and all the what-ifs are happening on top of each other all the time, simultaneously. She would take a stack of thin squares of muslin cloth. One on the next on the next. Each layer is its own history, the Cailleach would whisper gently.

At this, the Cailleach would release a single drop of indigo dye onto the topmost layer. See, she would tell her daughter. See? It bleeds through the topmost path and onto the next. In this way, so many things from the next world touch ours, and our world touches the layer beneath. You have the sight; the Cailleach would take her daughter's hands in hers. You will see the places where time touches other paths; you will see all the what-ifs and possibilities. You will know things that others do not, and they might fear you for it.

The Cailleach would pray that her daughter would remember the lessons, but they always forgot. They moved on to the world, and the enchantment garnered in their upbringing was lost to a mortal life. They lived long lives, longer than most, and never suffered from disease or illness. They healed quickly after an injury and heard voices in the trees. Sometimes they knew what would happen in the future; other times they saw things that were long past. Sometimes they were feared and other times worshipped. Some took on a quiet life, and no one saw their exquisite abnormalities at all. Some flaunted it and made elaborate shows of speaking with the dead and looking into crystal balls. But none of them remembered where they had learned to show the passage of time by dropping a point of indigo ink through a stack of thin squares of cloth. None of them remembered how to call the winds or why they knew the lyrics to ancient songs that seemed to quiet the fussiest newborn child.

And so the Cailleach carried on.

CHAPTER 9

THE BOY STANDING AT the door is holding Alice's hat. It's a silly top hat used in a dance performance when she was a child; Mum had thrown it out with the rubbish years ago. But here it was, in this strange boy's hands. The tag on the inside had neat printing: Alice Grace Kyles in block letters so familiar to Alice, she'd scarcely needed to consider the veracity of the boy's story. His name was Paul, and he had worked at Willow Caverns with her that summer. Now he was here, holding the tattered top hat in his hands.

Looking in his hazel eyes, partially blocked by a flop of rust-colored hair, she recognized him from a long time back, from that lane in Glasgow. Paths are funny things, Alice knew that, and she knew that slamming the door in his face and never returning to her cashier's job at Willow Caverns would set the entire world in a different direction. Still, she stayed glued to the same spot. Uncomfortable as he was, he held out the hat.

"Do you want it back?" he asked.

"Why would I?" she retorted. "I threw it out years ago. Would you like it if I brought you some of your own trash as a present?" He smiled at that.

"It's weird, though, don't you think?" he asked, an air of teasing in his voice.

He was a bit over a year younger than Alice and had just graduated from high school. Alice had just finished her first year of college, where she was studying to be a teacher. It was the last thing she wanted to be, but the engineering schools hadn't returned her queries, and despite her straight A's, they hadn't appeared with any scholarships. It was a good career, Mum had told her, it has stability; you can travel.

Alice was disappointed, and Grandmum Rowan back in Glasgow had written her saying she still knew people at the Women's Medical College even though she was long since retired. Alice had thought about it, but she did not feel the call to medicine the way her Mum and Grandmum had; she wanted to build things, she wanted to design and construct and work out all the minute details that others paid no never-mind to. But the United States, for all its myriad wonders, did not take kindly to a woman who wanted all that. The job at Willow Caverns was a summer job, and a good one at that. It paid $1.15 per hour. Alice kept it all in an account in town, an account that she hoped would pay for a deviation from the path that never seemed to stray too far from her line of sight.

She took the hat from Paul, the boy who worked in the maintenance office at Willow Caverns. She wished him a good day, and he grinned back at her. He would be arrested by the end of the summer. She didn't know it was going to happen, but it was no surprise to her. He and another boy got drunk after work, as many of the workers did, deep in the tourist caves: they would drink beer spiked with vodka—a cave party, they called it. Except this time they drank too much, and Paul and the other boy decided it would be funny to hide the cash box deep in the cave so the unpleasant manager would have a good start the next day. Their plan was to let him panic, then replace it when he looked away, making him think he was crazy. However, Paul passed out on beer and vodka in the cave, and when the manager found him there the next morning, he quickly made the connection between the missing cash and Paul. It didn't matter later, as Paul's friend and others tried to explain the joke. It wasn't funny, and Paul spent a couple of nights in jail until the manager dropped the charges on the condition that Paul never set foot in the caves again.

Alice wasn't sad. She knew she would see him again. Hopefully not too soon; she had some living to do before then. The tattered top hat was once again thrown in the rubbish bin. It had always been trash.

CHAPTER 10

ON THE NIGHT BEFORE *she knew her daughter would set forth into the world, Cailleach had inked the interlocking jagged lines of Ingwaz into her wrist, just as she had done for all her daughters.*

"But how will I forget all this?" the girl had asked in a pleading voice, not understanding.

The Cailleach had stroked her soft skin and tucked her unruly raven-black hair behind her ear. "It is the way it must be, mo sto'r. You must make the choice to remember; that is the way with our magic. It is an old story: you must cross the Lethe into the mortal world and leave it all your memories of this place. In time you may remember, but it is likely you will not. I can only leave you with this as a guide. You must follow the path on your own."

The girl had buried her head in her mother's chest, and the Cailleach had held her until she slept. She knew her daughter, when she woke, would begin to forget her face, her life, and her abilities. She would begin to doubt herself and be at the mercy of others for understanding. It was the way it had always been with their kind. The Cailleach herself had been the daughter of a hag even greater than she. She had been cast out of her mother's house and set on a lane. In time she remembered who she was and what she was capable of. She learned the old magic and how to live among men, yet apart from them.

She watched her daughter start down the lane as the sun rose the next morning. The jagged lines of ferocity brought together in unified peace burned onto her arm. The girl turned to wave and cast the Cailleach a confused look. It was already starting, the old hag thought softly. She whispered a prayer of protection and turned away from the inevitability of her loss.

CHAPTER II

JOHN KENNEDY HAS BEEN SHOT. Alice stood in front of her class. Her students were seated, books on their desks open to an interrupted algebra lesson. Overhead, the announcement blared on and on: the president of the United States has been shot as he rode in a car with Mrs. Kennedy. The school principal paused, more words to say but not sure how to say them. The whole world stood still for a long moment, and then a boy in the back of the room, a boy with a blond crew cut and blue plaid shirt, started clapping.

"Goddamn commie! That's right, he got what he deserves!"

The room sat in stunned silence for moment, and then the class erupted with whistles and cheers. A pimple-faced boy in the corner stood up, his arms raised over his head in some sort of prayer or celebration. The words from the overhead announcement had Alice in a deep state of disbelief and shock. She stood in the room, the cheers and chants of the overprivileged students surrounding her, and she felt her breath catch. She turned to the chalkboard and stared at the start of an algebra equation that had been interrupted by the speaker. A well of rage and anger coursed through her, and she slammed both hands on the board. The room went quiet, nervous titters emitting from the class.

"Shut up!" Alice's voice was clear and strong. "You have to live with this! You have to live your whole life with what you've done!" She paused; the stunned faces of the once-cheering students were slack with surprise. Alice didn't yell; in fact, her principal had talked with her on multiple occasions about being stricter, more assertive. But now she had found her voice, and the words poured out in an angry tumble. "Your whole life, when someone asks where you were when President Kennedy was shot, you get to tell them you cheered! You cheered like the little monsters you are! You live with that your entire life! You can't take it back; you can't undo it. Live with that."

Alice's whole body shook with rage and shock. Pimple-face sat down slowly, his face still red with its previous exuberance. An invisible wave of impact washed over her, and all of a sudden, Alice saw it all. She saw the pimple-faced boy sitting behind a cheaply made pressed-wood desk, his gut keeping his chair at a distance, his face red and strained with invisible pain. She saw him slump over, his pudgy, sausage fingers reaching out for help that was not coming. But today, the pimple-faced boy was just a fourteen-year-old kid echoing his parents' politics, a fourteen-year-old boy who had no idea of the impact of this moment. None of them did.

Alice looked around the room and saw their paths laid out before them. She saw the boy with the blond crew cut and plaid shirt dressed in a football uniform, a college crowd screaming and cheering as he ran. Suddenly he was knocked down, a pain shooting through his knee and back. The blond boy didn't know it now, but it would be the end of football, the end of walking without a limp. But now he was a kid who doesn't even really know what a communist is and certainly does not know what it is to lose a husband, a wife, a loved one. He was cheering for a concept he would never quite understand.

Alice took a deep breath, her left wrist pulsing irrationally. It was as though an invisible wall surrounded each of the children in front of her. They could not see their fates; they did not know their paths. The pimple-faced boy would live his life, kiss his wife, and go to work that day never knowing it would be his last. Maybe he would yell at his kids, or curse at his neighbor, or leave his wife with a crass word on that morning, never knowing it was the last time he would see them. The boy with the blond crew cut would not believe what the doctors told him; he would deny and deny and deny that his days of being hailed for his body were gone. He would remember the last time he had run the field, or climbed steps without pain, and never know it was gone forever.

But what hell would it be to know? The entire class was stock-still, as though time had stopped, as she pondered the horrific what-if of the hell those wretched creatures would suffer if they lived the next ten or twenty years knowing full well their fates and having no way to escape them. They would doubt it and think themselves mad; they might think her a witch and discount the lot; they might never join the football team, never take that office job. They would live in fear.

"I think she's gonna cry." The pimple-faced boy spat, his face twisted in a sadistic glee.

Alice brought her hands up and held the invisible curtain that saved the children from their fates for a long minute. The class sat mesmerized, their cheers silenced, their smiles erased. Then, before she could think too much on the matter, she brought her hands sweeping to the floor, and with it the layer of protection that had separated them from their paths was erased. The pimple-faced boy saw his whole life laid out before him; the blond crew cut knew instantly that he would be cut down. The others knew as well. They saw their future husbands never return from work, lost to the twisted metal of a car crash or another woman. They saw their own demises. Some were banal and ordinary, the running out of breath at the end of a long life. Some were more, a pulse sent through the brain at the wrong time that caused the entire structure to collapse. Alice realized what she had done and stood in front of the stunned and silent crowd, unable to take back what she had cast out in anger.

Alice made it into the hallway before the sobs escaped her body. She cried for the ugliness of the boy's cheers; for the loss of the promise of the young president; for his wife; for the little ones in the newspaper pictures, their daddy was dead and nothing would ever be the same. This was not a path she had seen coming, and it hit her like a brick.

The front office secretary came running up, her face contorted with concern and her own pain. She caught Alice right as she was about to hit the paneled floor. A great wave of numbness overwhelmed Alice, and she could barely hear the secretary call for help. A multitude of arms helped her up, and the next memory was of the nurse's cot in the office. A cool cloth was on her forehead. She wondered what had happened to her students, not sure she cared much. There was activity outside the door, a great scuffling about and footsteps here and there. Alice closed her eyes and let her body settle back onto the stiff cot. She hated the tight skirts and mini-heels she was expected to wear day in and out. The shoulders of her matching jacket were so tight that they make her feel as though she was in a straitjacket, and well she might be. She was barreling down a path and couldn't stop the momentum, but there were still adventures to be had, and no one, not even she, could know the outcome of such things.

She was leaving at the end of the school year; the arrangements had already been made for a year abroad teaching English in an American school in Venezuela. Her mother was decidedly happy about it, and Alice suspected that she wished she were in her place. On the other side of the door, Alice could hear muffled sobs and hurried voices. It hadn't been a nightmare; it was very real, and a hole had been ripped right across the country. She felt a strange numbness about what she had done to the children. But what had she actually done? Surely that wasn't possible; she had been upset and sad and shocked at their reaction. Alice felt a heavy layer of guilt and horror at her actions, and then remembered the boy with the blond crew cut in the back of the room who had started the cheering; he was so unpleasant. He leered at her every chance he got. Alice had tried to tell the principal, and he had laughed at her. He told her that boys had crushes on young teachers, and maybe she shouldn't wear quite so much makeup if she didn't want to attract attention. Alice was at a loss as to how to respond, considering that just the week before, the same principal had told her a bit of lipstick might help her look more professional. The boy had no regard for her or anyone, and if she had been too stern with them, then so be it. That was it, she decided. She had been overly stern, and now they would listen better.

This would pass, she repeated to herself as she reached up and pulled the cool cloth from her forehead. Soon, someone would be by to check on her, and she would have to act as though she were all right, but she was not. She would go back to the tiny apartment she shared with two other teachers, not a one among them able to afford their own place. Alice slept on the pullout sofa in the living room, and as such, had no space that didn't belong to all three of them. Her things were neatly kept in her rose pink suitcase in the hall closet. Her three skirt sets neatly hung beside her roommates' coats. Alice could feel the walls closing in there, but she knew that she would never have her own place here in Los Angeles. It had been her choice to move to such an expensive city, Aunt Polly told her; but still, she and Mum sent what they could, although between the two of them it still wasn't enough for an apartment, or groceries, or coffee even.

But it was getting better. She whispered that to herself over and over when she felt she would crawl right out of her skin. The Music Man helped a bit. It still felt a bit odd, calling him by his name, so she opted not to, skirting the subject, and soon he was known as Mr. Music to her roommates and soon to her as well. He had had a real name, of course, and he looked the same as he had back in Colorado Springs as he stood in front of the band room, leading the high school orchestra. Alice had been surprised to see him again; he was so far out of context, she hardly recognized his coal-black eyes and the graceful slope of his face. She'd met him again at a jazz club that one of her roommates had dragged her to for a supposed double date. Alice's date had left without her, and she hadn't cared. She'd stayed behind, watching Mr. Music play the trumpet on stage. It was a grand position to be in: she could see him, but he had no idea she was watching. She wondered if he would remember her. She had been first clarinet back in Colorado Springs, and he'd been full of teacherly praise back then. Funny, she thought, as she watched him lean back into a note, sweat sticking his white dress shirt to his chest. He hadn't aged much. She placed him in his thirties back in high school, and now, five years later, he had a streak of grey in his dark hair, but otherwise he had not aged.

To her surprise, he had spotted her from the stage as the set ended. A look of flirtatious surprise on his face, he crossed directly to her, shaking hands with the audience regulars as he passed.

"Alice Grace Kyles. As I live and breathe. I don't suppose you're old enough for me to buy you a drink yet."

She was, and they drank gin martinis until the bar closed. Alice had never been able to abide vodka since the days of the cave parties, no matter the mixture; it reeked of beer and body odor to her. Mr. Music and Alice stumbled out together, and somehow she found herself at the door to his tiny apartment in Silver Lake, the taxi pulling away before she could object. She fell into his arms, not caring what the world would think and knowing full well it wouldn't last and how perfectly terrible it would be if it did. She did it partially because she enjoyed the idea of the objections she knew would arise if anyone found out, because it was entirely naughty and wrong, and partially because the feel of his trumpet player's lips on her neck made every hair on her arms stand on end. A warm streak of fire ran up and down her spine, and her knees buckled underneath her.

Now they spent the weekends together at the dark club and, to the horror of her roommates, Alice slept over at Mr. Music's apartment so often that she bought a toothbrush just for the purpose. He paid her share of the rent on her shared apartment one month when the school had delayed their paychecks. Alice insisted on paying him back, but he had objected. Why didn't she just move in to his place? he said. Alice had laughed him off, and he had grown very serious. What if we got married? he had said. What if we did?

Alice had sighed, a great weary sadness overwhelming her. In his coal-dark eyes, she saw love and music and more passion than she could imagine. She also saw the gin martinis turn to overturned bottles of cheap wine. She saw the ugliness of reality, and she saw the harsh light through the cheap curtains of his tiny apartment. She saw herself used and bitter in a few short years. It wasn't a path that was any less or greater than what she knew she was heading toward, but it wasn't her path, and she could not follow it. She lied to him and said maybe—maybe after she returned from Venezuela. Mr. Music had looked hopeful and perhaps a bit sad, but they still spent weekend nights at his apartment, and even though their romance had cooled a bit, he was still a welcome respite. Today, as all this horror crashed down upon the country, she knew he would reach out to her, and she would willingly fold into his arms.

After a time, the door to the nurse's office opened, and the secretary stood silhouetted by the over-bright fluorescent lights. Her face was red and puffy from tears. The students had been sent home, she said. It was all just too much, she said, and started crying again. Alice stood too quickly and felt a rush of white light blind her for a short minute. She held the secretary in her arms as the woman cried. Alice's eyes were dry; she needed to start being honest with herself. She knew that now, but how to start?

That night, she broke it off with her Music Man. He didn't look surprised, and Alice had not cried. She went back to her shared apartment and curled up on her sofa bed as her roommates sat in stunned silence. No one seemed to know what to say or do. The world was ending with a whimper that echoed softly through the halls of the twilight kingdom.

CHAPTER 12

THE CAILLEACH HAD NOT *brought the cholera to the lost village, as was the story among the grown ones. She watched from her cave in the crags as it crept across the rough field grass, closer to the village. On the night of the full moon, she drew a circle in lamb's blood around the perimeter of the town. What the townspeople could not see was a wall that stretched to the clouds, invisible to the touch and permeable as water, but enough to keep them safe from disease. One of her many daughters lived in the town; long ago she had forgotten the roots of her childhood and now lived as a baker's wife with a gaggle of small children at her heels. The Cailleach watched her at times, hanging wash on a line stretched from tree to tree, milking an ancient cow, staring at the stars when she thought no one could see her. She looked like her father. He had been a sailor, dark and muscular. His daughter kept her length of curling raven hair tied back from her olive-skinned face. She did not look like the villagers, and they distrusted her for it.*

When the ring of blood was discovered, it was she they blamed. The Cailleach watched with growing rage as they tore her daughter from the farmhouse. She spat down rain and storm clouds as they tied her daughter to a stake in the center of town. The husband turned his head away, the children threw stones at their mother, and the Cailleach swore a bloody end to them all. The flames sputtered in the torrential rain; the wind destroyed their torches. Her daughter hung limply from the stake, sobbing quietly. The Cailleach undid her protection and watched as disease marched upon the town. Her daughter freed herself from her bonds and ran into the fields as the first among the villagers fell ill. They all died, one by one: the baker, the children who had never known anything but love and had repaid it with stones and hate. By the time the moon was again full, the village was full of rotting flesh. The Cailleach drew a new circle surrounding the town, this one to serve as a reminder of the cruelty of man. The farmhouse would never crumble, the stones would never fall, the flowers would grow in neat rows along the walkway, and no living creature would ever set foot there again.

CHAPTER 13

THE CORDS WOUND TIGHTLY around Alice's wrists cut deeply into her skin, and she could feel her fingers going dead, the circulation slowly ceasing. The rag around her head reeked of vomit, and she wondered how many others had stared into its filthy darkness. Her head ached something fierce from a steadily growing lump on the back of her head, where the policia had struck her from behind before grabbing her and binding her wrists, then throwing her in the back of the aging black sedan with the thickly tinted windows. Except it wasn't the policia, at least not the official ones. Alice had been in-country for nearly eight months now and recognized the official green-and-grey uniforms of the government policia, but that wasn't who ran Caracas. No, the policia wore the uniforms, but Alice had learned early on that anyone with enough guns could call themselves police. This wasn't any of those men. As she tried to make sense of the rapid Spanish, she knew exactly who this was: these were El Giro's men, a splinter group from neighboring British Guiana, a faction of the revolutionary party—the PPP.

"Donde estan los armas? Habla con nosotros pequeno parajo," a low voice growled in her ear.

Alice's Spanish was slow and clumsy, and the swift, angry words of the men on either side of her sounded like a wave crashing on her aching head. She shook her head and tried to speak as carefully as possible.

"No entiendo, por favor, no entiendo." She forced the words out, her tongue thick with fear and shock.

A hand on her thigh made her instinctively writhe away and smack at the pressure with her bound hands. The men exploded with cruel laughter. A voice from the front, in heavily accented English, broke through the din.

"Enough. Enough. We are not here to upset Tiburon's girl. I apologize. We need your help, Carino. We are looking for someone very close to you, and we believe you know where he is staying." The voice was silky, like the men in the telenovelas on the tiny black-and-white television in Alice's apartment. Lupe would be wondering where she was. She was home by now; the bus dropped her a block from their third-floor walkup apartment, and she was always home by 9 p.m. Lupe and Alice kept a close watch on each other; people had a way of going missing in the city, and the Peace Corps guys that regularly slept on their tattered sofa had repeatedly warned them about being out after dark. Even Alice, who with her dark hair and eyes could pass as Latina to most, stuck out as soon as she opened her mouth.

Alice knew that this wasn't quite so random. Tiburon, with his apple green eyes and dark curling hair, diver's body, and golden skin—that was why she was here. Alice had known better but hadn't been able to resist. She'd met him at a club in Caracas; she had gone with Lupe and a pack of the young Peace Corps workers who seemed to follow them everywhere. Most had been in-country for a year or more and were starved for a working shower, and they treated her and Lupe's tiny apartment like it was a five-star hotel. They were overwhelmingly kind, and from the time of her arrival in Venezuela, Alice had been happy to open her door and listen to their stories. The particular group they had befriended was here working with the prison system; they had been assigned to work with prison officials to improve conditions, but the backlash was escalating rapidly, and their numbers had thinned as threats from officials had grown louder and more menacing.

It was difficult to know whom to trust. The steadily brewing revolution in British Guiana had stirred the ever-present discontent in Caracas, and increasingly, El Giro ran the streets. But the policia spoke for the government, and neither seemed to have much of a qualm about shedding blood. The Peace Corps guys favored the People's Progressive Party, who some decried as Communists and by default supported El Giro, who claimed they spoke for the people and wanted the sort of reform that would turn the prisons from squalor—a modern-day oubliette—to a modern reformatory. Lupe favored the policia: she had grown up in this country although outside the city. She held no love for the revolutionaries, who she said preyed on the country folk, demanding tributes and payment, constantly questioning loyalty. She had exploded when she discovered that Alice was seeing Tiburon.

"He's not just PPP, he's worse. He's El Giro," she had cried. "He's one of the top men, and he'll be your death." With Alice unable to dissuade her, Tiburon was strictly forbidden from stepping near the apartment. Lupe did not want to be associated with him in any way. The Peace Corps guys had tried to calm her nerves, but in their own way had told Alice the same thing. He's not just a trabajador, they told her, he's a big deal. Don't trust him too much.

Alice heard them and understood the danger, but her heart had been Tiburon's since she'd seen him standing in the dim light of the club that summer night not long after her arrival in Caracas. His shirt was unbuttoned in the summer heat, revealing a firmly muscled chest. He'd seen her immediately, and his eyes had locked on hers. He had looked stunned for a moment, frozen, and then snapped back to his flirtatious smirk that made Alice's chest freeze for a moment every time, no matter the cause. They'd danced all night. The floor cleared for them, and Alice heard applause and cheers when Tiburon lifted her in a spin. The stars had been bright in the sky and everything had felt possible. In that sweet air, filled with the smell of arepas and saltwater, paths hadn't mattered. Alice forgot everything she was supposed to know about herself; she forgot that she was supposed to be plain and ordinary and safe. With Tiburon's strong hand on the small of her back and her hair fanning out as the joropo music rang out with perfect clarity from the stage, Alice was beautiful and free.

Even now in the back of the black sedan, with the stinking rag tied around her face and the charmingly threatening voice from the front seat telling her that they needed to find Tiburon and she should just cooperate and tell them where he was hiding, Alice wasn't sorry. Her heart beat slowly and methodically in her chest, and she felt a courage rise up in her that can only be born when one no longer cares if they live or die. This wasn't her path, but it was a terrifically more exciting ending than the one she had seen back on the lane in Glasgow.

"Vete al carajo." Alice spoke slowly and clearly.

There was a stunned silence in the car, and then the men exploded with laughter. Alice felt a rush of adrenaline course through her body. She expected the barrel of a pistol to press against her head at any moment, but instead the silky voice from the front responded.

"Calmate nina, I wouldn't expect Tiburon to run with a girl who didn't have agallas, but watch yourself. My boys are not known to be patient. We're taking you to see a friend of mine, and you might want to watch your tongue. He's a bit of a pendejo, my friend, and might not be so amused by you."

Alice swallowed her newly found courage and closed her eyes, blocking out the laughter of the men on either side. Things had moved quickly with Tiburon. She had met him the next weekend at the same club and they had danced, and Lupe had paced the floor of the tiny apartment until she had come home. A young Peace Corps man with shaggy blond hair had met her on the doorstep. Did she understand who it was she was getting involved with? he had asked. Did she understand how close he was to the top men in El Giro? She would become a target for the policia and the revolutionaries alike. He had a lot of enemies, he was dangerous, and it might not just be Alice who was at risk, but Lupe as well, and anyone who was associated with him.

Alice heard his warnings and walked past him into the tiny apartment so Lupe could tell her the same thing. She ignored them both and met Tiburon at the same club the following weekend; she walked with him down the streets as the cafés and bodegas swept their floors for the night, preparing to close. Tiburon talked an old man who ran a bodega into selling him a bottle of cheap wine even though they had long been closed. The man knew who Tiburon was and almost refused to collect any money, but he had pressed a roll of bills in the old man's hand that far surpassed the value of the wine. The man looked grateful and frightened. Alice heard the words of the shaggy-haired Peace Corps guy in her head and quickly silenced them. She walked with Tiburon's arm around her waist, and they sat on a dock overlooking the Guaire, the dark water gurgling beneath their feet. He popped the top off the wine, and they took turns sipping straight from the bottle. In his accented English, Tiburon told her about his home in Barbados, his mother, and the smell of couscous coming from the kitchen. He told her about diving for the myriad oil companies. He traveled out to sea as well as back to Lake Maracaibo, where the oil companies were king. Tiburon was paid to dive deep below the surface and cut the legs of the oil rigs when they were to be moved. The money was okay for the first leg but outstanding for the fourth, as it was up to the diver to dodge the falling equipment. Tiburon had already lost men on his crew, an accepted risk. Alice hung on every word, hoping this moment underneath the perpetual summer moon would never end. She felt her sense of self unraveling, and for the first moment in her life, she let go of her visions. Beneath the flashing dark lights reflected in Tiburon's eyes, his path was waiting to reveal itself to her, but she willed it away—not this time, she didn't want to know—and instead let herself fall.

He taught her to dive, first in a pool at a filthy rec center in the center of town, and then on weekend trips to Lake Maracaibo, weekends spent in a cabana by the shore. She let herself fall into his arms, knowing full well that she was intentionally ignoring more than she was seeing. But Tiburon's arms around her, his soft voice in her ear as they lay together at night, watching the stars, the feel of movement as he swept her around the dance floor: all these things were as substantial as a dream, yet they were enough.

Every so often she got a glimpse of the other side of this life. He disappeared for two weeks, returning just long enough to tuck a package wrapped in butcher's paper in Alice's arm, flashing her a smile, asking her to keep it safe for a couple of days. Alice hid it under the sink. Lupe never noticed, but she had grown cautious around her anyway so would not have asked questions if she had. The oil rigs were but one part of Tiburon's work, and Alice quickly learned that her handsome green-eyed man ran another side ring, running guns from Caracas to Georgetown in British Guiana, guns that were parceled out to the revolutionaries, the PPP and El Giro.

The black sedan lurched to a stop, throwing Alice forward in the space. The doors opened, and Alice heard footsteps outside the car. She wondered where they were and what would become of her now. The cold, sharp sensation of metal being pressed to her right temple made her body stiffen and her breath stop.

"What to do with you, parajito… what to do," an inky-dark voice whispered in her opposite ear. "Dead, and we might never find your young man, he might dive so deep he joins the other tiburons. But, I'm so sorry, poquito, we cannot just let you go either. We would look soft-hearted." At that, the voice chuckled, and Alice felt a sharp edge replace the blunt steel. "I think we'll take an ear. It will only hurt for a minute, amor, and our mutual friend will be sure to call us after that."

The steel pressed to her flesh, and Alice felt a thick line of blood trickle down her neck. She screamed in pain and surprise, but a stinking rag that was quickly shoved into her open mouth muffled the sound.

"Hush, little parajito, hush. This will only take a minute," the voice whispered.

The steel dove deeper, and Alice thought she might faint from the pain. Her mind went blank, and in the place of physical agony a white wall of rage rose before her eyes. She heard another voice whispering to her now, and she leaned forward, placing both hands on the concrete sidewalk as the knife sliced still deeper. With a stifled cry of anger and outrage, Alice funneled all her pain through her hands. Her left wrist pulsed and throbbed, and she heard the clatter on the concrete as the knife dropped. The night was suddenly still; the katydids in the trees sang, and she could hear the water on the shore. Blood was streaming from her aching ear, streaming down her chest. Alice wriggled her hands up from behind enough to jostle the blindfold, scraping it off on her shoulder, wincing at the aggravation on her injured ear. She looked to see the still forms of five men, all dressed in ragged suits and lying with their dark eyes closed, as if knocked unconscious by an invisible blow.

Alice freed her bonds by scraping them against the corner of the brick wall behind her, her left wrist aching and pulsing with each action. The stinking rag spat from her mouth and her arms and legs freed, Alice tried to stand but fell back. The blood from the side of her face had slowed, but her head was swimming nonetheless. Touching her head gingerly, she knew that while she did, indeed, still have an ear, there was a deep cut from the top down. She needed a hospital, and if she did not force herself to move, she risked passing out right there on the empty street, leaving herself to bleed to death alongside the men who had meant her harm. With a great effort, she took a step and then another and another still until she heard laughing and music from a veranda.

"Help!" she screamed and saw several surprised faces look down from the balcony.

As the hospital bus sped along the narrow roads and the medics held a wrap to her injured ear, she finally let what had occurred back on the dark street sink in. She had not touched the men; there was no way for her to cause them this sort of harm on her own. A power that she had felt before in lesser measures had flowed from her hands and overtaken them. She tried to feel guilt, but instead her mind flew back to that classroom full of students, what seemed like a lifetime ago, and the lowering of the veil and their paths revealed. Alice might have felt no grief for the unconscious men in the street, but she was overwhelmed with the weight of what she had shown a room full of children on that very dark November day. It had been real, and she had left them with the knowledge of how they would die as penance for their callousness. It wasn't fair, but even in shock and pain in the back of the hospital bus, she knew that fairness had little to do with what was right.

The policia came and questioned her in her hospital room, but she had no information for them and they did not seem surprised. When they awoke, the men did not remember anything of the evening; in fact, whole chunks of their memories had been wiped as if chalk from a board. They would never go back to their old lives again; never again would they recognize the faces of their loved ones. They were eternally in a fog, hints of remembrance and familiarity that did not connect to a solid reality. As far as the policia were concerned, this little American girl with a bandage on her head was hardly their problem. Thus, Alice went home to her apartment where the Peace Corps workers played quiet guitar and filled her tumbler with dark rum. Lupe sat beside her on the tattered sofa and held her aching hand. They lit candles; the electricity was out, as happened so often in this wild city. They sat, listening to the discordant guitar music, and Alice wondered about the stuff of fairy tales and how stories are told. She felt enclosed in this world and at the same time entirely separate.

Some months later, a riot at the prison erupted, and the shaggy-haired Peace Corps man with the gentle voice would be shot in the street as he marched with his fellow workers. The young man who had wiped the blood from her forehead and filled her glass would be hauled away by the policia as he rushed to his friend and never seen again. His family would write their congressman and send an investigator, but nothing would be found, no body to mourn, no closure. Lupe would leave the tiny apartment on Vente Quatro de Julio, moving back to Maracaibo, where she claimed the streets were safe. Alice would never hear from her again and so was left to hope that the city by the lake was safer than this city that seemed more dream than reality.

Alice had one last night with her Tiburon, before the riot and the death, before the end of all the things that had made the stars shine so brightly. Alice knew it was broken and not to be mended, and she had closed her eyes to the reality of life one last time. She allowed Tiburon's hands to twine themselves in her hair, working gently around her healing wound, and she let her body sigh as his lips traveled over her neck and down her chest. She smelled the salt-sweet scent of his skin and knew it was goodbye. He promised to write and she promised to return, all the while knowing it was a lie. She didn't want answers from him.

She wanted this dream of another life to last one more night, and in that she was given everything she wished for. When the sun rose, she reminded herself that her path laid in a different life, and on the spectrum of terrible things, this was a drop in the ocean. But it didn't make her feel any better.

Before she left Venezuela for good, Alice did one last thing. On the night before she was to board the plane to take her home, in a small shop not far from her tiny apartment, she had the symbol of the intersecting jagged lines inked onto her left wrist, a mirror of the tiny tattoo that adorned her mother's left wrist, a mark Mum never mentioned or wanted to discuss. Alice understood it now, and the power it carried frightened her. Her blood pulsed in time with the tattoo needle, and she felt the weight of the symbol, the certainty of completion—the idea that there was something much more grand in this life that she was meant for, and never to allow the mundanity of living make her forget that truth.

Alice returned home to the mountains outside Colorado Springs and swallowed the life she had almost had. Tiburon wrote letters in scratchy handwriting, telling her that he loved her. The postman read nearly every one before they were delivered to Alice, and soon the whole town knew of him. Of course, they only knew a shadow of what he had really been. Alice tucked the few photographs she had kept of him into an album sleeve and so made him a part of her family story, a reminder that she was not to be defined by such ordinary expectations. Eventually the letters stopped, and Alice had to say goodbye one final time to the sweet memory of sea salt air and what-ifs.

CHAPTER 14

AS THE CAILLEACH WAS *watching the villagers reel from the cholera, her daughter was running across the rough field grass, her face streaked with tears and her arms and legs aching. Bruises and welts from the stones, some thrown by her own children, the babes she had nursed and cooed to sleep at night, made every step a torture, but still she continued on, the madness and grief tearing at her heart and alternately filling her with an anger deeper than anything she had felt before. She had come to the village an orphan. She remembered nothing of her past; she'd been found wandering the lane by the man who would become her husband. She did not remember where she had been before or anything that might have happened. On the underside of her left wrist was a small marking in tattooed ink, the rune Ingwaz, interlocking jagged lines forming a diamond at the center.*

The old women of the village had clucked over her as they combed her tangled hair and gave her a small glass of mead to sip on her first night in the village. Fertility, they'd whispered, that's what Ingwaz means. Must have come from over the hill, the others whispered, where there was rumored to be a sect of women who worshipped the old ways. She must have been a priestess, or maybe just a serving girl, they whispered. Some, the elders among them, mostly men, didn't like her at all. Put her back on the road, they muttered; witchcraft it is, they said. But the girl was gentle and had an easy smile. She could soothe the fussiest babies, and although she did not remember how she knew, she could mix a compote of herbs to relieve fever. So she stayed, and the harvest was the best they had ever seen. The baker who had found her on the road married her, and her first child was born on the night of Eostre festival.

That child, and the others who slept in her arms and pulled at her raven hair with their tiny hands, had plucked stones from the ground and thrown them as the elders lit the flames of the pyre. The daughter of Cailleach raced on through the brush as the rain and wind raged behind her. Her grief and shock now turned to anger; she carried the forgotten magic with her as she ran, eventually reaching the sea where waves rose up to meet her, crashing down on the shore in a storm the likes of which the sailors had never seen. In that moment she remembered; she remembered the enchanted world of her childhood and the drops of indigo dye permeating all the layers beneath. In another world, on a level below this one, perhaps, she was milking the goats while her children played in the morning sun. Her life was simple and utterly complete. She looked to the sky and cried for her mother, her lost family, and the storm raged on around her.

The old women had not been wrong so much as they had been incomplete. Ingwaz was the rune of the Norse god Ing, a peace-bringer who would end a war that had raged for generations among the Viking people. The interlocking jagged lines were the birth of a new whole made from parts that had formerly been too ragged to fit together. Ingwaz did symbolize fertility, but on a scale that the old women in the village had no ability to comprehend.

CHAPTER 15

ALICE WAS STATIONED AT her cashier's desk at the entrance to Willow Caverns. She was earning summer money that she hoped might be enough for an apartment of her own before the school year started again. She was teaching at a neighborhood junior high school in Spring Falls and sleeping in the tiny bedroom where she had grown up, Mum and Aunt Polly treating her like she was still a teenager. So as soon as summer vacation began, she went back to her old boss at the caves and signed up to man the cash register again. The younger kids still had their cave parties and invited her to join, and although she had but a few years on the oldest of the lot, she felt a world away from them all. Some of the crew from her previous life there were still around. One of the accomplices in the great money-box heist that had led to the boy Paul's dismissal from Willow Caverns was still cleaning the floors and hanging the lights in the limestone caves. He hadn't been caught, and Paul hadn't turned him in. He came to her early in the summer, a grin on his face: Did she want to give

Paul a call? He was still single; some might say he'd been waiting for her. Alice had smirked and laughed. She knew what was to be, but no sense in rushing things.

On that early June day, the road to the cave was empty, and Alice slipped a newspaper listing out from under her clipboard. She had several apartments circled: one-bedroom units; a space they were calling a "bachelor," and she grimaced at the description. Landlords would be hesitant to rent to her, a woman alone. She shuddered as she realized that Mum would probably need to co-sign her lease, and that would raise more questions than Alice cared to answer. Even in Los Angeles, at the apartment she shared with her roommates, the girl who had held the lease had to get a co-sign from an uncle. If she were a bit older, then it wouldn't be such a fuss; she'd be labeled a spinster schoolteacher, and no hint of scandal would follow her. But as it stood, the idea of a woman living alone, unmarried, needed validation. Alice wondered if the world would ever change, but she didn't see those sorts of paths.

A long black car was winding its way up the hill, and Alice snapped back to attention, shoving her newspaper back under her paperwork. It proceeded slowly, and Alice saw that there was a second black car behind it and still another behind that. Curiously, she watched as the car in the front paused and then proceeded, as if unsure of where to go. All three pulled in perfect unison into the closest spots in the nearly empty parking lot. As though a cue was signaled, eight men wearing identical black suits jumped out and jogged to the cashier's booth, flanking either side. Alice was flustered, confused by the formality of the scene.

"Sir?" she managed in a voice that sounded too high-pitched to be hers.

"One moment, miss," a dark-suited man began and then paused, watching the middle car intently. "One moment, miss," the man repeated and then stepped back, arms behind his back, matching the others. The rear car door opened, and a man in a jaybird-blue suit and red striped tie jogged past the black-suited men, straight to Alice, who found herself staring at the young senator from New York. His wavy hair was brushed back from his chiseled face, and his sky-dark eyes crinkled at the edges as he offered a genuine smile. Alice was struck dumb. She stuttered a bit of nonsense that made him smile wider, revealing perfect ivory teeth.

"Excuse us, miss," he said in his clipped New England accent. "We have found ourselves with just about thirty minutes to see a few sights." He paused, waiting for Alice to respond, and then softened his voice to add, "Didn't mean to give you such a shock."

Alice shook her head, trying to find her voice. "It's not. No need to be sorry, sir."

He reached up and pushed his dark brown hair off his forehead. "Is this a sight you would recommend?"

"No," Alice blurted and immediately regretted the word. The senator laughed, the sound free and natural. "What I mean, sir..." Alice continued, fighting the stunned paralysis her vocal cords were experiencing. "What I mean, sir, is that if you only have thirty minutes, I wouldn't do this. Most of the caves are false, anyhow; they made the structures out of plaster to trick the tourists....It's all in the lighting, and they're terribly ordinary really." Alice found her previous paralysis wearing off, and she stopped herself from rambling further.

The senator nodded, a grin set on his handsome face. "Thank you, young lady. Your honesty is refreshing. If I might ask, what would be a better use of our time?"

Alice returned his smile, a deep urge to freeze this moment forever in her chest. "I would drive up to the red rocks if I were you. I can draw you a map. There's a spot at the top that, especially this time of day, catches the light, and, well, if you want to see the beauty of the place, that's what I would do." She locked his eyes for a long moment, and then set about scratching out a map on the back of a Willow Caverns information sheet. Alice reached forward and held out the map. The young senator smiled a slightly lopsided grin and handed the map to the nearest suited man, who nodded as he received the paper. Then he reached out and clasped Alice's hand in his. The feel of his smooth, cool skin made the blood rush to her head with so much momentum that it blinded her for a moment. His path hit her in a flash of light. She saw the young senator with a flood of people, their eyes rapt, the sort of hope that hadn't been familiar enough in this time. She heard his voice booming, promises of his brother, and promises of peace. She squeezed the senator's hand tighter and heard the clatter of metal and saw the flash of fluorescent lights; she heard screams; a young man, a kitchen worker, covering the senator's body with his own, tears falling from his eyes; men in suits clamoring; chaos and blood, so much blood. She saw the emptiness of his young wife's eyes. She saw the end of an era; she saw those same crowds standing at attention with damp eyes, leaning against one another for fear they might fall.

The senator's smile faded. "You all right, miss?" He asked gently. Alice nodded slightly. "You've been a great help. Can I ask your name?"

"Alice. Alice Grace Kyles," Alice whispered, not letting go of his hand. "Sir, I want to say thank you, and… " Alice lost the words. There was nothing she could say that would change his path; she didn't know when or where, or even how. She stuttered slightly. "I just hope it all has a reason, all the things that happen. I need to believe that sometimes."

He reached his other hand forward and enclosed hers. "I think I know what you're trying to say. Thank you for your condolences; my brother touched more lives than he could possibly know. I hope to live up to his dream."

"Thank you, Mr. Kennedy," Alice said softly, her voice quavering slightly.

He winked at her, his dark blue eyes catching the early summer light, and with a final shake, the senator from New York thanked her once again and jogged back to the open door of the waiting car. The three long black cars pulled around in a U-turn back to the road and headed up the highway toward the Garden of the Gods. Alice watched until they were no longer visible. Her eyes were dry and her throat was raw, the weight of knowing hanging on the edge of every cell in her body. She would see the young senator again from the back of a crowd of people in a bit over a year's time. He would decide to run for the presidency, and the nation would celebrate, sure of his win. Alice would stand at the back of the crowd, her eyes dry and throat raw, the futility of knowing slowly building a callus over her heart.

CHAPTER 16

THE DAUGHTER OF CAILLEACH *slowly discovered her sway over men. She discovered she could stop them from talking with a wave of her hand and force them to forget by fixing a gaze. She took a cabin long abandoned on the rocky cliffs that overlooked the sea. Using the magic she had forgotten for far too many years, she ringed her house in lamb's blood and spoke words that had not left her lips since she was a girl. No one could enter this space without her permission; no one could even see it, and if they did, they would quickly forget. She moved the cabin out of the reality of man and just off to the side. She enjoyed watching the men and women come and go in the little fishing town on the shore. She loomed over them like a great black bird, not intending harm but not protecting them from ill will either.*

One night she witnessed a shipwreck off the coast. The screams of the men filled her ears and fixed her to a spot overlooking the sea. Dozens of tiny boats, men rowing madly, made their way to the sinking vessel, but most were too late. A handful of dying men were plucked from the water; the rest drowned, their bloated bodies bobbing back to shore with the tide.

The daughter of Cailleach felt no duty either way to help these creatures that had shown her no mercy so many years ago. She was as young now as she had been then; time had ceased aging her body and mind on the day she remembered. She could stay like this forever if she chose, half in and half out of the world, watching the slow progression of time and the little men and women who inhabited it run from here to there so busy with their lives.

For a great stretch of years she did just that. She watched the children of the seaside town grow to be women and men; she watched them die surrounded by newly formed versions of themselves, the grandchildren and great-grandchildren of the sailors who had survived the sinking ship so far back in the town's memory that they told it as a folk story now. She remembered the feel of her babys' skin on hers. She smelled the sweet, clean scent of their hair, and when she closed her eyes, they fixed their gaze on her in perfect love. She had no idea what had come of them; she had run and never gone back. The whole of the country had been taken out by cholera or plague, and she supposed that little village that had been her home was no exception.

The daughter of Cailleach knew the price of what she wanted. She knew that like her own mother, the Lethe ran deep and strong around her cabin. She knew that a day would come when a child born in this place would cross the invisible waters and forget, and all she could do was hope they remembered who they were one day. She knew she would never see them again, and still the urge was building up in her like a drumbeat. She also knew that the promise of Ingwaz, the certainty of a conclusion, and the peace it would bring would manifest itself in one of their line; the pinpoint drop of indigo ink was working its way through the clean squares of muslin cloth, and the daughter of Cailleach knew it would pass through her and on and on.

One day at the end of the Eoster festival, she walked the path down to the village and out onto the docks. A particular man caught her eye. His hair was the color of a burning ember, a hint of fire hidden in his beard and eyes. She watched him go about his work, and as the sun went down, she watched as the other men went home to their lives and children. But not this man; he stayed behind, alone. He was young—too young to have married and had children of his own. The daughter of Cailleach approached him slowly; it had been a great number of years since she had spoken to any living person. Later, as he crossed the ring of lamb's blood, he said he felt as though there was a stabbing sensation in his chest but also a lightness, and the daughter of Cailleach knew it was a death of sorts and she ought to feel remorse, but she did not.

Their daughter was born on the longest night of the year, when darkness overtook the land and the winter winds howled in with the frozen sea. The daughter of Cailleach sent the man back to his village on the same day she felt the life within her. Everyone thought he'd fallen overboard, maybe hit his head; he didn't remember a thing about where he had been, but he couldn't stop staring at the cliffs overlooking the town. Many years later, after he had married a girl in the village, when his own children were old enough to go exploring, he would warn them away from the spot. They wouldn't listen, but as they approached the overhanging cliffs, one would swear he saw a little cabin, and another a witch, and another still a great black bird in the trees above. They would run home with wild stories about the sea cliffs.

But on that Winter Solstice night, the daughter of Cailleach was alone with her fire-haired daughter and the howling wind. She would raise her to hear the voices of the mer-creatures deep below the surface of the water. She would teach her how to raise the wind and drive the waves away from the shore. At night she would sing her the lullabies that soothed the fussiest baby, and they would pick the herbs from which you could relieve any fever. She knew, as the girl grew older and her eyes wandered more and more often to the town and life below, that she would leave. She had *fire in her eyes like her father, and she would not stay any more than the daughter of Cailleach had. As the girl grew to be a young woman, the daughter of Cailleach stroked her child's soft hands and inked the symbol of Ingwaz on her left wrist. The girl cried and asked why she had to forget, and the daughter of Cailleach soothed her tears. "It is our way, mo sto`r," she whispered as the tiny pinpricks of ink seeped into her skin. It was the only thing she could give her before she crossed the Lethe and entered the world of man.*

CHAPTER 17

THE GIRL WITH THE *fire hair looked back at the little cabin on the edge of the cliff. A beautiful woman stood in the doorway, her raven hair rippling around her face, and she stared at her as though she were familiar. The girl waved a bit and kept walking on the path to town. With each step it became more and more clear that she knew neither where nor why she was going. Suddenly panicked, she looked back to the cabin only to see nothing there. The girl rubbed her temples; a stinging pain was setting in, and a desperate fear that she had made a terrible error. On her left wrist she saw the marking: two jagged lines intersecting. It was familiar, but she did not know why, and the sight of it made her want to cry. Still, she walked down the hill to the village.*

With no money and no understanding of what was happening around her, she sat by a fish market looking around uneasily. It was a man with dark fire-colored hair and matching eyes that first took notice of her.

"Do you know where you are, darlin'?" he asked gently.

"I can't remember a thing. I was up on the cliffs, and now... " she murmured.

The man let this sink in. He took her to his cottage and introduced her to his wife and brood of fire-haired children.

"Your eyes are like sea stones that wash up from the deep," the woman had said kindly. "You look as though you could be related," she said, frowning, looking from her husband to the girl.

They called her Coira after the colored sea stones, and the little ones took to her immediately. She sang songs that calmed them in their fussiest moments and knew how to mix a compote of herbs to soothe their coughs and fevers. The melodies were familiar to the man, but he could not place where he might have heard them. Every once in a while, the two of them would fix their eyes to the sea cliffs and share a faint memory of a flash of raven hair and the soft hum of long-forgotten melodies.

CHAPTER 18

PAUL HAD BEEN ARRESTED AGAIN. This time, he got smashfaced at a pub in Colorado Springs and tried to walk home. "At least I didn't drive," he kept telling her, and Alice's resentment was not a bit abated. He walked to the row of houses where he rented a back room with the meager earnings he claimed from his multitude of part-time jobs. But this time, he hadn't found the correct back door. When the knob refused his key, he put his fist through the window, reaching around to undo the lock. The neighbors had found him passed out at their kitchen table the next morning, the blood from his sliced hand pooling on the tiled floor. They called the police, and he was taken first to the hospital and then to a cell where he was allowed to ride out the raging hangover brought on by whiskey and cheap beer. Alice was the first phone call he made, and she promptly hung up on him. The month prior, he had been let go with a warning from the Colorado Springs police after a bar fight that had resulted in a sprained wrist for Paul and a broken nose for the other participant. Alice had sworn that she would never speak to him again if he kept up this nonsense. He had promised, his rust hair cut short now but still long enough to catch the ruddy accents in his hazel eyes.

He was going to turn it all around, he said; this was it, no more, no more. He was leaving for boot camp in the Air Force the next month, and this was it. Alice hadn't waited to hear more, just slammed the phone down and stomped down to the stone tea table and buried her head in her hands. Mum had joined her after a time, bringing two mugs of steaming lavender tea.

"I figured you might want some refreshments for your party," she said with the utmost seriousness.

Alice looked up, her eyes dry. She already felt as though the parts of her life that set it apart from the mundane were past.

"He's a young man, love. Young men are far too often eejits who act more bairn than man. Is this really what's got you ragin'?" Mum said kindly.

Alice accepted the tea and shook her head. Mum didn't talk about the paths, although she didn't discount the spirits. She left a small dish of salt in the windows when the winter moon was full and left a plate of sweetmeats and honey in the kitchen window every All Hallow's Eve. Dornoch Dreams had been Arthur's favorite, and although they never spoke of it, Alice wondered if she blamed her in some way, even if for knowing before the others, for seeing the path.

"It's not Paul, Mum—well, maybe it is a bit. What guarantee do I have that it will ever be any different?" Alice clutched the tea, letting the warmth seep into her cold-tinged fingers.

"I suppose you don't have any at all, love. What about him makes you give him the time of day anyhow? He's not nearly as handsome as the poor boy you were fixing to marry all those years ago. You remember him, surely. Saw him at the grocer just last week. Still single, that one, back from Vietnam. From what his mother tells me, he's taking it pretty hard, living back at home, not working. He asked after you. He heard of your Latin man, think he was more than a bit jealous. Hell, I think we're all a bit jealous of that one." Mum chuckled a bit, and Alice caught her smile, feeling the misery in her chest unclench a bit.

"That poor boy was wretched slow, Mum," Alice groaned. "You know I had to tutor him through most of his classes even though I was two years behind him, right? He once asked me why FDR didn't just cheer everyone up if they were so depressed, and I think he was actually serious."

Mum giggled, a magical sound that floated through the air, a rare sound from a woman who rarely wore a casual smile.

"Your Latin man hasn't written in a bit," Mum observed.

Alice shook her head. It had been about six months, and she knew better than to tell Mum what had led to the silence: a letter from a woman in Barbados with a grainy photograph of three skinny children who had her Tiburon's apple-green eyes and copper skin. A plea to take them to the USA; she didn't care about the affair, she wanted them to go to school, to eat a regular meal each night. If Alice married her husband, he could move to Colorado, USA, and take the children with him. Alice had perhaps been able to see this ugly truth during her time in Caracas, but something inside her had always warned her against looking too closely into Tiburon's heart. She rubbed her ear that still held the trace of a scar and locked her gaze with Mum's. It was hard to say if she knew or not; Mum always seemed to know without being told, and Alice was quite accustomed to her quiet acceptance of things, which would leave most gob-smacked and shaken.

Alice had written to Tiburon, telling him it was over, that she couldn't keep doing this; she couldn't keep living the lie of a promised future together. She couldn't take him and his children to Colorado, USA. He had responded with an envelope containing a single photograph. A photo of Alice standing against a pale wall. She was wearing a white sleeveless top and black skirt, her hair piled high on her head, her face turned slightly to the camera, dark eyes unreadable. A smile played on her lips. A single phrase had been written on the back.

"No su su, love, come back tomorrow-day."

Written in Bajan slang, it was most likely the end result of a night of dark rum, and it didn't entirely make any sense, but Alice hadn't minded much. It was enough for her to say goodbye, but she kept his photographs carefully tucked in the album, no matter the path that had been laid for her. So Alice just gave Mum a melancholy smile.

"Come on, Mum, can you imagine the looks on the neighbors' faces as you introduce them to your new Latin son-in law? They're already scandalized to pieces by you as it is." She added a teasing note to the last bit, and Mum smiled back.

"Let them talk," Mum said simply, standing and collecting the empty tea mugs. "Come, you best go collect your young man. You know his mother will let him rot in that cell, and sleeping on a neighbor's table isn't exactly a felony. The Welsh simply aren't like us, you know."

Alice frowned. Sleeping on a neighbor's table wasn't a felony, but it wasn't a good omen either. Mum was right about one thing: Paul's strict-as-nails mother, a Colorado transplant from a

Kansas farm and a long Welsh line—which was, to Mum, possibly the worst thing to be—was unlikely to show any mercy. That would be Alice's job from here on out.

CHAPTER 19

ALICE IS GETTING MARRIED, and this time doesn't feel any more real than it did with the poor, stupid boy back in school. It had started with Paul sitting on the stiff, scratchy sofa in the living room, which was strictly reserved for guests and not at all the same as the deep-pocketed soft furniture in the alcove off the kitchen. No, the living room was for formal talks and serious business. Paul was back from boot camp, his rust-colored hair shorn close to his head, making her realize that the shy, sweet boy who had brushed his flop of hair out of his eyes as he stood on her doorstep and handed her an old hat was ages away. He was leaving for Vietnam in two weeks; his poor vision and flat feet meant he would be spared active combat, so he was to be trained as an air traffic controller, helping the military planes to land at a base set deep in the countryside of Vietnam.

"We should just go ahead and get married," he had said.

Alice had laughed. They were hardly even dating; she had bailed him out of jail for his petty transgressions twice now, and the rest of the time she had spent trying to convince herself that he was worth the effort. There was something else, though, that kept her listening when she knew she should close the door, a deep-seated urge that rose from her heart and spread out to the tips of her fingers. She found herself watching women with their babies and could almost imagine the smell of their skin and feel their tiny fingers intertwined in her hair. She could see herself lying at night curled around a sleeping infant, pushing her in a stroller as the fall leaves fell from the trees. It was an oddly primal urge that overpowered all her other senses. It caused her to look past the obvious and see Paul as a whole. He was smart, frighteningly so. For all his surface irresponsibility, he remembered every single thing that he read or was said to him. Later, Alice would regret seeing this as a benefit when he threw back long-ago spoken words in anger, his lips curled back in cruelty.

But as she sized Paul up, categorizing his benefits and weighing the risks, she didn't see that. Alice saw that their children would be intelligent and gentle. He had an almost magical quality with animals. Stray cats would wind their ways out of their hiding spots to rub against his legs and follow him down the sidewalk. Once, when they had been walking past a tiny pet store in a shopping center, a red-and-green parrot that had been placed in a wretched display in the front, chained to its perch, protected with only a small sign warning not to touch, jumped off its perch, fluttered its useless wings, and landed on Paul's shoulder. As it landed, it began to squawk a series of complaints, and Paul had looked at it as though the senseless noises made perfect sense. It had continued until the pet store owner came running, bawling Paul out for grabbing the bird. No one could convince him otherwise, and Paul had laughed about it later. What was the bird saying, Alice had asked teasingly. What does anyone say, he had responded sadly. The bird had been unhappy and needed to tell someone about it.

Paul gave his pocket change to anyone who asked. Alice wrinkled her nose and asked him how did he know they weren't just going to spend it on liquor or drugs? "What do I care?" Paul had responded. "That man needs money, and I have some. Now we both have some." Alice had, from that point on, kept a few quarters or even a dollar in easy access and gave it without question to the men who sat on the corners in Colorado Springs, some back from the war, some staring into space, their minds left behind in a jungle in Vietnam.

But Paul also had a streak of wildness that scared Alice. His missteps were blamed on his tragic Welshness by Mum. But the thing that drove his actions had nothing to do with being Welsh, or a man, or even an inability to see the consequences of his actions. He was destructive, and in the moments when he lost track of himself seemed to revel in the abandon. His eyes changed color and narrowed so that the pupils became pinpricks of darkness. He could be cruel, and Alice had seen him turn his anger toward his strict Welsh mother and thin-lipped sister. He had older brothers as well who had moved from the family home, leaving Paul there. The mother and sister attended Mass twice a week and reminded Paul at every opportunity that he was bound for hell. As for himself, Paul had no use for the Church. He could not speak of it without his face clouding over with what Alice grew to understand was the precursor to his alternate self, the one who hurt others and lashed out at the world around him. But now he was out of his mother and sister's house; he was a man on his own. Fresh out of boot camp and bound for war.

"Let's just do it," Paul repeated to Alice as he settled back on the scratchy sofa, a beer in his hand and an unreadable smile on his lips. "Look, if I get blown up in a jungle next month—which, let's face it, is likely—you will get all the benefits and money from the government. Otherwise, it's going to Mom and Sis, and Jesus, you can at least appreciate the tragedy in that."

Alice had reached over and slapped his leg a bit harder than she intended. He'd winced slightly, but the grin on his face widened.

"So it's a financial arrangement, is it?" Alice had countered. "You really work a number on the romance, don't you?"

"Firstly, ouch. Secondly, not entirely. We get on well don't we? We were meant to be together; I've known that since your hat nearly ran me off the road. You believe in signs; I know you do. Who else are you going to marry? Your aunt will sell you to the Mennonites if you hit thirty and aren't hitched, and you scare the hell out of everyone else, except maybe that boy your Mum told me about from school… " His voice was light, but his eyes had taken on a tint that made the hazel look more gold than brown.

Alice had closed her eyes then reached over, taking the beer bottle from Paul's hands and helping herself to a swig.

"That boy is brain-damaged, and truth be told, he didn't have much up there even in the best of days," she muttered. She was stalling, the precipice before her looming ever closer.

"Alice, we could build a life together, you and I. We believe in the same things, we want the same things. If I make it back in one piece, we can build our own house away from here, live our lives without anyone telling us what is right or proper. We can have a family. And if I get shot the moment I step foot in-country, you'll be set and you can do whatever you like. We all win." He took both her hands and stared deeply into her eyes, not blinking, and Alice felt the old path, the one she had glimpsed back on High Street, open back up, and with a deep breath and full knowledge of the counter of light and dark, stepped off the precipice.

CHAPTER 20

ON THE DAY OF *her twelfth year, Muireall kissed her mother and father goodbye and left for the ancient temple in the highland hills. Her escorts were young women wearing blood-red robes that covered their faces. The townspeople feared them, and no one would meet her gaze as they walked the lane out of town and to the road. The journey would take days on foot; that was what Mum had said. And we won't see you for many years, perhaps never again, Mum had also said with tears in her eyes. Muireall hadn't understood why she had to go, but Mum and Da had been insistent. The smallpox was creeping around the harbor, Da said. The ships that came from England were ripe with it; a cargo ship full of bodies sat far off in the water, no one daring to touch it. It would sit there for years, the bodies rotting into the frames, the abandoned ship eventually sinking into the water from disuse. Already, the fishmonger and his wife were dead of the pox, his children left wandering the lane. No one would take them in for fear of infection.*

Mum knew how to mix medicines, but her poultices and compotes only eased fever and rashes; they couldn't fix this. She fussed over Muireall and Da, and Granddad and Grandmum too. Muireall's cousins were all men now and worked on the ships. Mum made them drink solutions made from berries and herbs she found on the cliffside whenever they came around. Muireall had heard stories of her Mum, how Granddad and Grandmum had taken her in when she was a girl. No one would believe it to see; Mum and Granddad had the same fire-red hair and coral eyes. That was how she got her name according to Da: Coira, for the sea rocks. Mum still claimed not to know what had happened to her before she ended up in the village, but Muireall wondered why she knew the things she knew. No one could heal like her; no one understood the plants and herbs like she did.

The elders mistrusted her and had once even raised a case for witching, or so Da told Muireall. They were to hold a trial over a poultice she made for the reeve's son. The boy had had the flu, and death was certain, but the next morning he had woken as though never was a brighter day. His fever broken, there was no trace of illness about him. It was witchcraft, the elders said, and Mum was taken in for questioning. However, before the trial could begin—as Da told Muireall late at night as he tucked her into bed—before the trial could begin, a wave larger than any that had ever been seen rose on the sea, a storm the likes of which even the most seasoned sailor had never known rose up, and the town was near destroyed. The chief elder who had raised the complaint was killed, drowned and his body drug out to sea, not even a proper burial. No one had much interest in pursuing it after that, Da said. The townspeople love your Mum; she's saved so many lives here, he had said to Muireall, and no one thinks her a witch except the old man who drowned in the storm.

Muireall wept when Mum and Da told her she was to leave. It's a school of sorts, Mum had said. All women, and you'll learn so much more than we can teach you. You will learn to read and how to make medicines. Mum had paused then and leaned in to Muireall's ear: you'll learn how to call the winds and songs to ease the fussiest child, and how to raise the sea, and the order of the stars. But you can teach me that, Muireall had sobbed, holding her mother tight. I can't, Mum had cooed in her ear, I can't. I don't remember.

So the women in the blood-red robes had arrived and waited while Muireall kissed her mother goodbye. Her wrist ached a bit from the sewing needle and the ink. It's all I can leave you with, Mum had said with tears in her eyes; I think mine came from my Mum but I cannot remember fully. This is all I can give you, she said as she inked the interlocking lines of Ingwaz onto Muireall's left wrist. To remember us, Mum had said. And as she walked down the lane with Mum and Da watching, Muireall was glad of the sting; it would remind her of who she was and what she was capable of.

They walked for days, stopping only to sleep. The robed women never spoke. Muireall would learn later that they were neophytes and not permitted to speak for any reason. They prepared meals of grains and plants. They stopped as the sun went down and began at first light. Muireall, not accustomed to the trek and desperately missing her family, wept as she walked. The robed women placed their hands on her shoulders and moved her along gently. Muireall missed the rosewater scent of her mother's fire-hair. She missed how Da made her laugh and the magical sound of it. Her mother had been herding her brothers through the market when he saw her, as Da told it. He had been an apprentice in the blacksmith shop; later he would take over the trade and come home smelling of sulfur and soot. As Da told it, though, on that day, he saw Mum with her fire-red hair trying to move this legion of little boys through the market, and as soon as she'd set them one way, they'd go another. He fell in love fast, Da said, and they were married in the summer under a canopy of meadowsweet and sage.

The women in the blood-red robes never spoke but nodded when Muireall had shown them the ink mark on her left wrist. She was expected at the temple, that much she knew. And so she walked, the first of her kind to leave her home without the weight of Lethe. Deep in her cave by the still black waters of the underground lake, the Cailleach stretched her ancient joints and felt the bones crack and shift. She had long ago left behind an appearance that was human in nature, and she now existed in a feral state, a form more true to earth than to man. A faint ripple passed over the glassy surface of the water, and the Cailleach knew that something far more ancient than she had been was set in motion. A girl bearing the mark was entering training in the ancient arts; underneath the soil, the ley lines felt the vibrations and hummed in celebration. The intercrossed, jagged lines of Ingwaz, inked on her wrist by her mother as she had done to her daughter and hers after and hers beyond that—all the ancient marks borne to a line of women more ancient than the Scottish hills—began to beat a rhythm, slow and solid, that would become a rallying cry. The ancient peace promised by Ing and the bringing together of the worlds of man and hag were in sync at last. The Cailleach rose to her feet in a ragged motion and pulled herself through the bowels of the cave and into the night air, where she blew a soft breath at the stars; in them all the love she felt for her daughter passed to this girl who walked with the ones who would teach her the ancient arts.

Muireall stopped and stared at stars with her robed escorts. They sparkled with a brightness that was extraordinary to see, light jumping from star to star in a silent song. Muireall felt the marking on her wrist vibrate in allegiance to the rhythmic beat of the night sky. The red-robed women exchanged glances and lowered their eyes to Muireall humbly. They walked on, Muireall suddenly comprehending why she had to leave her Mum and how important it was for her to reach her destination.

"Come," she said, and the robed women followed.

CHAPTER 21

THE TEMPLE WAS SET *into the highland hills, the entrance a great wooden door that opened outward to reveal an entrance hall carved into the mountainside. Lit by torches that never dulled, the effect was as terrifying as it was magnificent. On that first day she arrived at the temple, an ancient woman with silver hair and deep-set green eyes greeted Muireall. The women in the blood-red robes knelt in reverence as she approached, so Muireall did the same.*

"The hills have been talking, little one. The hag Cailleach sends her blessings with your arrival." The woman's voice was broken and stilted but carried a power that reverberated through the hall. She took Muireall's hand and led her through the structure. Sleeping halls for the neophytes, rooms for lessons, meditations, and spell-casting. Practical areas such as food preparation and an underground river where the laundry was washed. The temple had existed for thousands of years, and for thousands of years the neophytes had become priestesses and worked to maintain the balance of peace in the world of man. Wars nonetheless raged across the land.

Muireall would learn the art of herbs and plants. She would learn how to summon the rain and to bring the mist when one needed to cause confusion. Muireall would remember much of this rather than learn, and one night, after Muireall had been with the temple for many years, the old woman would lead her out the wooden doors and tell her the story of her great-grandmother and eventually how her mother had come to the fishing village with no memory of where she had come from. The old woman would tell Muireall the story of Ingwaz, the rune on her left wrist, and how her bloodline was even more ancient than the temple itself. She would tell her that she and her daughters would be the peace-bringers that had been foretold in all the ancient writings.

Muireall felt her body vibrate as the old woman spoke. And some time later, she would take the vow of a priestess and the symbol of the sisterhood would be inked onto the back of her neck at the very base of her hair. Laguz, a simple straight line with a downward hook at the top, the symbol of the underworld, of magic and the power of those that understood its purpose. The next morning, she would don the indigo robes of the priestess and leave the temple. A mission set upon her by the old woman. A task that only Muireall could perform, one that meant she could never return to the temple that had become her home.

A new Laird sat on his throne in a castle on the sea cliffs. He was young and brash and full of war. He fought his way to the throne, killing indiscriminately, locking away anyone who questioned his authority. He stood in the way of another who was meant to lead. A war would be fought, and many would die if something were not done. This new Laird sat in his seaside castle and listened to the wind. He believed in signs and the old magic, and so when the priestess appeared on his door in indigo robes, bearing a potion that she claimed would bring him long life, he happily drank it down. It was foretold, he said to the hooded woman. I am immortal and will rule this land until the very end.

It was not to be, though. For as he spoke, he choked and gasped for air. His pages and advisers ran to his side, but it was far too late. His immortality had been cut short; the war he would start ended before it began. The priestess in the indigo robes had vanished before any of the court had realized she was there at all.

Muireall understood the meaning of the words the old woman had spoken to her. Her bloodline was the very thing that would bring about the peace promised by Ingwaz. Her daughter was born on the Solstice night, just as Muireall had been and her mother before her. The father was a nobleman in the new Laird's house, and the three lived peacefully and comfortably. Muireall taught her daughter all she knew, and as the daughter became more woman than child, Muireall sang softly to her as she inked the symbol of their blood onto her left wrist. She told her the stories of the Cailleach and the Temple. She taught her daughter the arts of saving and ending a man's life.

It was a new time, and the girl took her talents and studied the new medicine being discovered and unearthed by the men around her. She used her gifts to open the doors that had stood closed to women, and soon her name was known far away. A healer more skilled than any in the land, a formidable presence with her dark eyes and raven hair, passed on from her great-grandmother. She walked through disease and death and never it touched her; it glanced off her as it had her mother and all the women who had come before her. She lived a long life, practicing the arts of the ancient women mixed with the knowledge and science of the day. She had one daughter who, upon her grandmother's insistence, received the mark of Ingwaz as she grew into adulthood. The vibrations in the ley lines reverberated around them, and the power of Cailleach echoed in their hands.

CHAPTER 22

PAUL HADN'T WRITTEN IN nearly three months. In the very beginning, Alice had received two or three letters at a spell. Knowing exactly how slowly the military mail ran, she hadn't let herself worry; when it did arrive, there would be a small bundle of letters, proof that not only was he okay but also that he had not forgotten the life they planned on building together. They were inconsequential for the most part, descriptions of the Vietnamese countryside. He was at an airstrip on the edge of a jungle. The Air Force dropped supplies for the troops as well as the Vietnamese civilians caught in the crossfire. Paul was an air traffic controller, out on the strip, directing the fighter planes and helicopters. He wrote about a constant ringing in his ears, which Alice knew in a few years would become near-total deafness that would leave him dependent on hearing aids. His writing was poetic; it was a side of him that Alice had no idea existed, and, in the moments when she was doubting her decision, it comforted her some.

I lie here underneath the stars. They seem to shine brighter here, but that might just be for lack of distractions. I spent so much of my life to this point seeking out distraction, that it's alarming to have to spend so much time with no other way to look. I have nightmares nearly every night; the night is full of things that I cannot even begin to describe. A base medical unit is nearby, and we transport the wounded that are headed to the hospital in Saigon. Alice, you haven't seen this sort of hell; I pray you never do. I'm not sure how we are supposed to feel about each other. I realize now that we hardly know each other, not really. I've only ever known that you fascinate me and have since the day I saw you.

Alice kept the letters in a box at the back of her closet. She read them out loud sometimes, in case Arthur was listening. She still whispered to him at night, even though Arthur was long gone; his spirit had never been among the ones who walked the house. Alice still heard the raps in the hallway when she laid her head down to sleep at night. The furious pranks still occurred. One day, a man who Mum had hired to fix a broken plank on the back deck went running for his truck, leaving his tools behind and the job half-done. Mum had chased him out of the driveway, where he paused long enough to tell her that someone had blown in his ear, and there were children giggling all around him as he tried to work. Mum tried to explain that it wasn't anything to pay any mind to, but the man had none of it, never even returning for his tools. Mum had just sighed; it was hard for people who didn't know the house to accept its ways.

But Arthur wasn't one of the voices in the shadows; he never had been. Alice kept his bed in clean sheets and neatly made. She wouldn't live here forever, and she worried about who would care for it when Paul returned and they moved to a place of their own. Mum did not speak of that; she never spoke of Paul at all if she could avoid it. Aunt Polly and Mum would sit at the long table, drinking the thick, strong tea that she and Mum favored, both whispering about things that they didn't think Alice could hear. It was as though she were a child again. But she was a woman, worthy of sitting at the table in her own right, but she never took her place beside them. Instead, she preferred to stay in her childhood room and whisper the day's events to Arthur.

The wedding had been small and odd. Haphazardly planned to beat Paul's departure for Vietnam, it was held after the Sunday service in the same way that Alice's ill-begotten plans to the poor, dull-witted boy back in school had been meant to happen. Paul's mother and sister sat in the front row. Two of his brothers joined them, the oldest now off in Vietnam himself, the younger leaving in another month, and the other exempt for reasons that Paul refused to talk about. On Alice's side, her Mum, Aunt Polly, and a handful of churchgoers who lingered on after the Sunday service. Alice wore a short, boxy ivory mini-dress with a lace collar and matching high-heeled ivory boots with a sprig of heather in her hair. Mum had been horrified, but it was Alice's one rebellion. The entire affair was only happening because Mum had heard Alice and Paul talking marriage in the living room. She had begun planning, but this time no one would pull the plug. Alice held her breath, swallowed the rising ball of doubt in her gut, and stepped forward. The dress was one of her own making, modeled after one she had seen in a magazine. Alice wasn't a prize at tailoring, but could operate the foot-pump sewing machine well enough and the dress looked nearly professional, so long as no one looked too closely. The elderly pastor who had been a rabbi in his past life had since passed, and his son was now leading services at the tiny church. Alice remembered him as a quiet boy who seemed to melt into the very walls, but now he stood at the head of the church, leading the service and smiling kindly at Alice.

Mum had made some calls, and as she and Paul walked down the aisle to the common room where a wedding dinner waited, a lone piper dressed in a clean if somewhat ragged suit played "Highland Cathedral." Later during the dinner, as the plates of roast beef and mash were being passed around, Alice would ask her Mum where she had found the man, who had swiftly poured himself several shots of Jameson and was now dozing in a chair by the rectory. Mum would tell her that Colorado Springs was short on pipers, and beggars can't be choosers, and not to go too hard on the man; he was Irish after all, and it was hardly his fault.

Paul had had too much to drink, and Alice had to walk him into the rented room that Paul's mother had given them as a wedding present. Two nights in the rented room by the mountain lake. It wasn't exactly a honeymoon, but it was what it was. Alice had some money saved up and had wanted to go on a proper trip, but Paul had talked her out of it. He was leaving in a week; he didn't want to go out of town even for a night, so the rented room by the lake was all there was to be. Paul passed out nearly as soon as Alice deposited him on the bed. The next night, he had sat quiet and moody as they ate dinner at a rustic wood table in a café by the lake. Alice had felt a pain in the pit of her stomach and hadn't stopped him when he abruptly stood and walked out the door. She'd found him some time later sitting on the shore of the lake. He was due to report to the Air Force base in Colorado Springs in five days' time, and his hair was cut in a tight crew cut, making his eyes appear alien huge. She sat next to him, watching him gaze out at the rippled moon reflection.

"You're going to come back. I can't explain how I know it, and you wouldn't believe me if I tried, but I can only tell you that you don't die in Vietnam. You come back home," Alice said softly.

Paul had turned his head to face her, his expression unreadable and his hazel eyes cloudy.

"I know the stories about you, Alice Grace Kyles—I mean Coslet. Creepy. That's what the guys at the cave used to say about you. Pretty, but creepy." He gave her a half-smile.

"Oh, that's a lovely thing to tell your bride on her honeymoon," Alice retorted, but she was secretly relieved to see the fog that had surrounded him since he'd awoken with a fierce hangover lift.

"It's true. Creepy. One of the guys said that every time you were around, the lights would go on the fritz, and he would have to go back in the cave and change the bulbs again, even if he'd just done it. Another said you'd answer questions he hadn't asked yet, and you didn't even seem to know you were doing it. One of the girls, the blond one with the weird nose—Janice? Janet?"

"Marty. Her name was Marty. But you're right about her nose, it was weird," Alice muttered, her lips twitching in a grin.

"Marty, that's what I said," Paul said in a teasing voice. "Marty said that one day you told her how sorry you were about her boyfriend, but he was a dog anyway, and she'd find someone better."

"What's creepy about that?" Alice asked. She remembered Marty with the nose that ended in a stub, much like a piglet's. Her boyfriend had also worked at the cave and smelled of sausages and dirt.

"At the time you said it, nothing had happened. Marty told us that she had no idea what you were talking about. And then a day or so later, she found him making out with that dark-haired girl with the lisp in the lower cave during a party," Paul replied.

"Huh," Alice said softly. "Well, it wasn't creepy; anyone could see that coming if they were paying attention. But I don't think that girl had a lisp normally; she had braces on her teeth."

Paul leaned forward and reached with his hand to stroke her neck, his fingers wrapping themselves in her loose hair. Alice immediately felt a bolt of electricity fly up her spinal cord, the first hint that this strange boy could ever be a lover.

"I know all sorts of things, Alice Grace Coslet. I've been watching you for longer than you know. I had no idea how to approach you and no clue you'd ever pay me any mind. I don't know how to do this, and I am scared to go to Vietnam. But if you say I'll come home, then I believe you. I don't know what home means, and I suppose that scares me even more than the bloody war." His pupils were wide, the blackness threatening to engulf the thin line of hazel entirely.

"We'll figure it out together," Alice whispered.

That night Paul had fumbled his way into bed, and amidst comically wretched awkwardness, Alice found herself in his arms, and the path that had showed itself to her so long ago shone clearly.

But now Alice lay on her childhood bed, listening as she had always done to her Mum and Aunt Polly gossip at the kitchen table. She stared at the ceiling and wondered if the paths she saw were true or merely one of many possibilities. She wondered if there were another world where Arthur grew to be tall and strong. She wondered if there were a path in which she and Tiburon lived together in a house in the countryside, away from the wildness of the city. She wondered if there were a world where Paul didn't come home, and yet another in which she was allowed to live her life alone, not bound by the decisions of others.

As she closed her eyes, Alice drifted into a dream: a stack of thin squares of muslin cloth sat upon a dark and ancient tabletop. A woman with raven hair and ageless eyes looked up at her and smiled in a way that was both kind and terrifying. Without speaking, the woman dropped a pinpoint of indigo ink onto the stack, and Alice was struck with an awareness of time and reality. She saw all the paths occurring on top of each other, simultaneously, none greater than the next, but different. She felt the black ink on her left wrist pulse in time with the universe, and the raven-haired woman smiled and turned her own left wrist to reveal a matching mark.

As Alice slept, a force of nature shifted in her cave far away, across the ocean in a place long forgotten to the memory of man. Come home, the creature whispered, come home. Alice woke, her heart calm and certain. She was bound for greater things; there was a memory just out of reach that grew ever closer. She needed to be patient and watch the signs as they unfolded, not be distracted by the obstacles of an ordinary life.

CHAPTER 23

SEVERAL GENERATIONS OF DAUGHTERS *passed, and the line began to forget. The mark of Ingwaz was no longer inked into their left wrists, and soon bits of ancient knowledge began to become hazy and distant. The traits of their entirely mortal fathers began to outweigh those of their ancient matriarchal line. Their innate ability to hear the voices of the dead ones or see the patterns of fate in a palm or a flash of a thought became parlor tricks and seen as oddities as opposed to the link to a noble and fearsome hag. The vibrations set forth by Cailleach became fainter, but not quiet entirely, and in her cave hidden well among the lowland hills, Cailleach still felt the presence of the line of powerful women that she had created. She had stopped taking mates after the cruelty inflicted upon her daughter in the village so long ago, and the farmers and townspeople no longer left her gifts of salt or dried meat. She still observed their harvests and daily life by gazing into the still, black water that kissed the shores of the underground lake. She sat by the shores of the black lake: a great, molting reely-mouse who hardly drew breath and meditated upon the persistence of truth that she had always known lay intertwined in the jagged lines of Ingwaz, and while it was somewhat dormant, it was far from dead.*

By the time Moira Blair was born in the Saltmarket District of Glasgow on the first night of winter, it was no longer an accepted truth that she would be the only daughter. In fact, she came into a world already occupied by two older brothers. The vibrations of the ley lines ticked in the rhythm of Moira's blood, and she was seen as an exceptionally odd child. While her brothers would scream and run in the fields outside of town, chasing the red squirrels and anything else that moved, Moira could be found building a fairy mound out of bindweed and thistles. She talked to herself often, although the conversation was largely one-sided as though some invisible person was answering back. Her mum and dad exchanged looks and let her go on about her ways. She was a child, after all, and no harm came from childhood oddities.

As Moira grew, she learned to read the runes from an old woman who lived on the lane. Everyone knew the old woman's brain had been rotted away by the scarlet fever, and Moira's mum worried about her daughter spending so much time with the sad old thing, but it was an ultimately kind gesture to give such a woman company, so they allowed it. Moira knew the woman's brain was far from rotten but didn't tell anyone, as the perception allowed her a great deal of freedom. The old woman had told Moira on their first meeting that she had a gift, and that she could teach her how to use it. Moira had started visiting her every day, and every day they would talk and study. Moira learned to read the rune stones and the lines on the palm of a hand. She learned to speak to the voices without making a sound and to summon the spirits of the deceased by going into a meditative state. The old woman taught Moira everything that she had suspected in the fields as a child: that the fae and the witches that everyone said were stories existed in a world just beneath waking life, and they watched human comings and goings at their will.

One day as Moira was walking down Bell Street on errands for her mother, she saw a flash behind her eyelids. A well-to-do woman in the dress of the gentry was crossing the street when a horse and carriage came roaring around the corner, run free from its owner. The woman stopped still, terrified, and the horse reared up, coming down upon her. Moira could see the thick, dark blood mixing with the Scottish mud and hear the screams of the onlookers as they watched helplessly from the sides.

The vision ended as fast as it appeared, and Moira stood dazed. Just then, a woman in the same upscale dress crossed in front of her and started into the street. Moira moved on instinct and ran to her, grabbing her by the arm and pulling her back to the side. The woman let out an outraged cry that was cut short as a horse and carriage ripped around the corner and barreled down the now-unobstructed street. The woman stared at Moira for a moment and stuttered. Moira's hands and body were shaking uncontrollably, and she dropped the packages of bread and cheese she had just bought and ran home.

The woman, as it turned out, was the Lady Elsbeth Crane, eccentric wife of a wealthy merchant and trader. Her interest in the occult arts was seen as an embarrassment to her husband, tolerated by her friends, and ignored via healthy bribes to the local polis. After the incident in the street, Lady Elsbeth set about finding the girl who had seemed to predict the runaway carriage and saved her life. It wasn't difficult; the cheesemonger remembered to whom the package belonged, and it was thus that Moira Blair, an odd daughter and unknowing heir to an ancient line of hags, came to live in the great house of Lady Elsbeth Crane as adviser and counsel.

Moira read the cards for Lady Elsbeth and her curious friends. They asked her to call the spirits of their fathers, mothers, and dead husbands. Sometimes the spirits answered; sometimes all Moira could do was offer counsel that did not require the sight but rather a kind heart and common sense. She became known among the gentry ladies of Glasgow, and soon the curious and wealthy from Aberdeen, Edinburgh, and even London were lining up at Lady Elsbeth's door for a chance to see the young medium.

She never resorted to the cheap tricks of the day. Other women and men called themselves mediums and planted tricks to make it appear the spirits were among them. They used fishing line to pull tiny bells hidden in the corners of the room; they rigged tables that would flip and spill the candles and incense to the ground so it looked like an other-worldly tantrum. But Moira Blair never needed such novelties. She had an assistant flash a refracted light back and forth before her eyes, and she would feel herself cross the mist into the next world. Once there, the dead ones would congregate, waiting their turn to speak. She would call out for him or her in question, and with rare exception, they appeared. They talked to her of wrongdoings, last words of love, and occasionally the scurrilous actions of the living who were asking for contact.

In time, Moira Blair lived in her own grand house on Cathedral Court overlooking the Necropolis, with a vast stretch of land fanning out behind the manor and a caretaker's cottage nestled deep in the woods on the edge of the land. She still read the runes and always came to rest on one in particular: the jagged, intersecting lines of Ingwaz. She suspected that this symbol had a far greater meaning for her than she would ever know. She taught her own daughter the art of summoning the dead and reading the lines in the palms of hands. She taught her that with the right sort of concentration, you could summon the wind and rain. Moira Blair lived a long life, free from illness and full of peace. Her daughter grew up learning the old ways as they existed in a new world, and far off in the lowland crags, the Cailleach celebrated the resurgence of the ancient energy.

CHAPTER 24

THE LEMON-YELLOW AUSTIN-HEALEY SPRITE is gone. Alice stood at the shipping dock for well over an hour before a gruff officer came huffing over and told her the car was nowhere in their stock. Forms, he said. There were forms for her to fill out, and the Air Force would investigate its loss and compensate her if its loss was found to be their fault. However, his dismissive air made Alice quite sure the Air Force would most certainly not be finding itself liable. Still, she filled out the forms and caught the bus back to the base, all the while trying not to think about how she should have been speeding down the roadway with the top down on the sporty little roadster that she had ordered from London before she left for the UK. Alice had never had a car of her own; the little Dodge she drove back home was a hand-me-down that her Aunt Polly's gentleman friend had rebuilt. It hiccupped and coughed and frequently refused to start. Upon learning that she was to be living on the Air Force base outside a town gloomily called Seven Mile Bottom, she had taken her savings and splurged. The lemon-yellow convertible was horribly indulgent, but at the time Alice had been feeling very sorry for herself, so it was a small price to pay.

But now it was gone. In another month, Alice would see an officer with stars lining his uniform speeding across the base in her lemon-yellow Austin-Healey Sprite. Paul would try to explain to her through her rage that it wasn't uncommon for the officers to pilfer property from the shipping dock. It was her fault, Paul would say, for ordering such a flashy car; what exactly did she think would happen? Alice would shoot daggers with her eyes and add the injustice to a growing list of grievances. But right now, as Alice climbed off the bus, flashing her identification at the gate guard and walking down the narrow path to the married airmen's housing, she had other grievances to stew on. She had been here about three weeks, and already she was beginning to see that life on the base was not going to work. For one, she had a job, which set her apart from nearly all the wives who had been following their husbands around from base to base. Alice had been employed by the American Secondary Academy in town to teach junior-level science. She was due to start in a week, and as it stood, she would have to take the eternally slow bus back and forth, adding three hours to her commute.

Alice had already looked at listings for rooms in town. She could afford it, and that fact irked Paul more than he was willing to let on. Alice didn't much care what angered him right now. Her arrival in this desolate part of England had been onerous to say the least. Nearly ten months had passed without any communication from Vietnam. Alice had found herself in the Air Force base's Family Affairs Office seeking any information they could give her. He was alive, she knew that; the military was swift to deliver that news but didn't seem to care much about the total lack of correspondence. Finally, they had tracked him down to a base hospital. He had been suffering panic attacks following an incident at the airstrip. No information was offered about the incident or how long or why he was at the base medical center. A month later, he would be transferred out of Vietnam and sent to Seven Mile Bottom in the UK. The official reason was listed as "psychological stress," and it made Alice hold her breath for a long moment, remembering the vacant stare he had had so often and the flashes of anger and rage he tended to.

Alice talked to him over the phone the night he arrived in England. Mum was sitting in the next room with Aunt Polly, pretending not to listen. Paul was quiet, refusing to explain his utter lack of communication for nearly the past year. With negotiations befitting business colleagues rather than those of two newlyweds, Alice settled for the fact that she would move out to join him in the UK at the end of the school year. School ended in three months; she would come to him. He didn't object, but in the same breath, he never asked her to come. Alice didn't care; she had taken this leap and was tired of being a pretend wife. She was tired of the sad looks she received from her coworkers and the neighbors when they asked after her husband. In the beginning, she knew the gossip had been that she was pregnant and had married before Paul left town for the sake of her reputation and that of the unborn baby. Soon enough that rumor was quashed when her belly refused to swell, and after nine months and no baby, the clucky neighborhood hens were forced to abandon their theory. Now they just assumed that she was a desperate, sad girl who had latched on to a man who was never coming home. Alice was tired of the sideways glances and whispered talk.

She was going to meet up with him, and they would live together as a family whether he liked it or not.

But now, as Alice sat in her dank, concrete-walled base cottage, she questioned her judgment. She had seen this part of her path, but it had been foggy, and now she realized that her gift was more unreliable than she cared to think. Paul had met her at the airport in London on the night she arrived, a crooked grin on his wan face. He looked dreadfully thin, and she could see his cheekbones and collarbone protruding in places not previously obvious. He pulled her close and hugged her for a long minute. "It's good you're here," he had said, "it's good." Alice had felt heartened that she was doing the right thing. She would make a life for them here, a real marriage. But she realized now, three weeks later, that it wouldn't happen on the base. Her lemon-yellow convertible, her one indulgence, was gone, and she all of a sudden felt the sleet grey walls closing in on her in this base cottage that didn't hold the heat and left her constantly shivering.

There was a particular listing that had intrigued her: a Miss Lettie in an old manor-turned-boarding house, walking distance from the school and with a view of the heath and countryside. She had spoken with Miss Lettie over the phone and had already made an appointment to come and see the room the next day. Paul had stared at her, his eyes clouding over. "So you don't want to live here with me then, do you?" he had asked accusingly. "What exactly was the point of you coming all this way, just so you could live off the base and away from me?" Alice had pointed out that the hours he worked left him little time at home anyhow, and he could easily join her on his days off; it was only an hour's drive to town. However, for all his ostensible cold anger, Alice had whiffed an air of relief in his reaction. She was beginning to suspect that he was hiding more than she could ever guess from her. He had been here, in-country, for nearly four months by himself, and the other families in the base housing had looked shocked at her arrival. Paul hadn't told them he was married, they said, embarrassed. Alice suspected there was more that they weren't telling her, but she didn't push for information, unsure if she really wanted to know.

He still had not talked about Vietnam or what had led to his rather hasty transfer. His record retained the label of "psychological stress," and Paul was required to speak with a base psychologist each week. He didn't tell Alice what they talked about, nor did he explain what had led him to stop writing. It hadn't been just Alice; Paul's mother and sister had sent with her with a bundle of letters that Alice was to deliver to him personally. They had tried to send them to him while he was in Vietnam only to have them returned. No explanation or communication. Alice at least had the satisfaction that Paul hadn't returned her letters with the post. Had he read them? she asked him on that first night she arrived in England. "Yes," he had answered simply.

The English summer was in full swing, which meant that it rained slightly less than usual and the air might hit 70 degrees at the peak of the day. Alice was always cold here; she had forgotten this part of her childhood. She thought of her Gran, who had passed away years before, her long silver braid over her thin shoulder and her eyes a bright honey-brown in Alice's memory. All those years ago, Alice's Mum had tried to get the old woman to move to the United States, but she had refused. "My home is here," she had said. "My work is here." Alice missed her with a pain that tugged from the innermost part of her heart. She had not seen her since she was six years old, but she had kept every letter they ever exchanged. Gran's scratchy writing, in which she tried to relay the history of their family, the lineage of their tartan, and even an obscure relation to Katherine Howard and Anne Boleyn. Alice had Gran's braid in her small cedar chest; it had been sent to her after Gran's passing along with a quilt that smelled like sage and Scottish mornings. What she wouldn't give to go to Gran now, ask her what she should do, how she could make this marriage into something worth having.

The next day, Alice would take the bus to Miss Lettie's manor house and would fall in love instantly with the dark-paneled walls and the older woman's round apple cheeks and kind eyes. Miss Lettie would insist that Alice take the very best room, the one next to the lavatory. "A young woman, just married and wanting to start a family, would want the very best room," she would say and then turn to brew a pot of thickly scented tea. Alice would feel warm for the first time since she'd arrived. Paul would join her on his weekends, but it would never be his room, not his house. He would always be "the other" in this place. Alice would know that she didn't need Paul to have what she wanted from this match; the family she was creating was stronger than this ill-fated union.

CHAPTER 25

MISS LETTIE POURED A HEALTHY shot of brandy into Alice's tea from a silver flask that she kept in her side pocket.

"Calm yourself, love. No little French girl is worth this sort of fuss." She spoke quietly, calming.

Alice was shaking, her hand barely able to keep from spilling her spiked tea all over Miss Lettie's red-and-silver oriental rug. She had arrived home an hour ago, and Miss Lettie had found her in the garden, pacing and cursing under her breath. After coercing her inside and out of the English rain, Miss Lettie had covered her shoulders with a thick handmade quilt and planted her on the stiff sofa in the formal sitting room and insisted she join her for a cup of tea.

"Is Paul due here tonight?" Miss Lettie asked cautiously.

Alice shook her head. She didn't tell the old woman that Paul would be lucky if he was ever welcomed back to her room. More than ever, she saw her room in this house as hers—her space alone that had nothing at all to do with Paul.

"Start from the beginning, love; there's nothing I love more than a good story, and I suspect that anything that would get a Scot this angry is a good story. Take your time, there's plenty of tea." Miss Lettie sat back with her own brandy-tea, looking expectant.

But where to start? Alice sighed. She had gotten the post two weeks ago. Nathalie was the name of the sender, the sister of Sylvie, who had been involved with Paul since his arrival in this country nearly five months ago. The news that he was cheating wasn't so much the shock. That news carried the weight of inevitability, a sinking feeling in her gut that more than anything confirmed her suspicions. The part that had knocked her vision white for a full minute and had given her a pounding migraine headache was that Nathalie wanted Alice to come to their house on the south side of London and have tea with them. They wanted to meet her, and they wanted Sylvie to meet her. "To what end?" Alice had asked over the communal phone in the hallway, knowing full well that Miss Lettie and most of the residents were listening to the entire conversation. The house ran on gossip, and this sort of fuel was not to be squandered.

"To what end?" Alice asked. "To show her," Nathalie had answered simply. "She's young, she's foolish, and she won't listen to us, but she might listen to you. Please," Nathalie said. "Talk to her; talk to us."

So Alice had found herself outside a stone-step walkup in South London on a Wednesday afternoon. She stood on the walk in rain that wanted to be snow but couldn't quite commit to sticking to the ground for longer than a moment. Her toes were numb in her leather boots, and the wool scarf that she had knitted from Miss Lettie's pattern was scratching the back of her neck. She had worn a smart, slim-fitting pine-green dress with matching jacket, the sort of thing that she imagined Jackie O would approve of. Alice knew it caught the light in her eyes and accented her raven-dark hair. She stood on the walk, pulled up her sleeve, rubbed the intersecting jagged lines inked into her wrist, and straightened her spine. She was a warrior; she could do anything.

Before her hand even reached the door, it flew open, and a hobbit of a woman stood in the entryway. She was well under five feet, and her wiry black hair was screwed into a wide bun at the back of her head. Her face was round and red-cheeked. She immediately grabbed Alice by the hand and pulled her inside.

"Vous devez etre Alice!" Her voice was like nails on sand board. She then turned and called into the back room. "Faire bouiller la bouilloire! Nathalie! Do you hear me, girl?" Turning back to Alice, she offered a wide smile, revealing yellow- stained teeth. Alice nodded, confused as to what she should be doing.

"Hello, I apologize for the state of the house." She said with an accent so thick that Alice found herself having to sort out the words a moment after they were spoken. "Come, come and sit down."

The woman led Alice to a low sofa that appeared to have a thick coating of golden dog hair on it. With a sigh to her smart evergreen dress, Alice offered her black wool jacket to the woman's waiting hand and sat down. The owner of the golden fur came loping across the room and buried his snout in her chest before Alice could object.

"Luc! De! Vers le bas!" The woman shouted across the room, but the golden-faced creature with matching eyes didn't seem to care. He sat on Alice's toes and panted, his face one of utter delight. Alice was suddenly very glad for his presence; at least this made some bit of sense. Nothing about this meeting did. Why had she agreed to meet this girl that her husband was planning on leaving her for? She sighed as the woman reappeared, followed by a slightly taller carbon copy of herself. Nathalie carried a tray with a kettle, four cups, and a small plate of biscuits. Nathalie offered Alice a weak smile and set down the tray.

"Sorry for the dog. He is not usually so friendly with strangers. He must know you are a good person." She indicated an empty cup, and Alice nodded as the woman took a seat in a fur-covered armchair adjacent to the sofa.

"You have met my mother, Beatrice," Nathalie said, and Alice nodded. "We are most grateful you agreed to come, I know it must be so genant… I mean, odd, uncomfortable." She looked uncomfortably around the room. "My sister is scared of meeting you. She is thinking you are angry with her."

"Then she would be right. That being said, please tell her I did not come here to fight," Alice said in a steady voice, every moment feeling more and more like Jackie O, a figure on an entirely different plane than these women and their stale ginger biscuits. Nathalie nodded, stood, and left the room, leaving Alice and Beatrice to sit uncomfortably together, only Luc for company. For his part, Luc regarded Alice with his great golden eyes and seemed to be saying that he understood the ache in her chest and that it was going to be all right. Alice reached out and impulsively kissed his snout. He responded with a solid lick to her face. Beatrice wrinkled her brow, obviously confused by the exchange.

Nathalie reentered holding the hand of the infamous Sylvie. Alice took a long look and then switched her gaze back to Luc so as not to speak her thoughts. Sylvie had by far received the middling portion of looks in the family. She stood perhaps even shorter than her hobbit mother, and her healthy hips and bosom gave her the appearance that she could in fact be rolled like a barrel rather easily if one was inclined to do so. The family's signature wiry black hair was loose and hung in a straight clump to her waist. Her eyes were bright and dark, and her skin shared the red-cheeked splotchiness of her mother and sister. Alice ran her fingers through Luc's fur and swallowed a string of curses.

For the solid part of an hour, Nathalie asked Alice about her life in the United States, where her family was from in Scotland, what she thought of the English fog, and had she ever been to Manche? Of course she hadn't, why had she asked that? Would she like more tea? Never once was Paul mentioned, and never once did the mysterious Sylvie speak a single word. Alice answered all the questions, stubbornly directing all her answers at Sylvie, the girl's face growing increasingly crimson. Finally, as the clock on the wall struck a quiet chime, Alice stood, and to Luc's dismay, swept the coating of golden fur off her dress.

"I must be going," she said in a stately voice, still channeling her inner Jackie O. Beatrice and Nathalie stood; Sylvie remained in her seat. Never had Alice, at a grand 5 feet, 4 inches tall, felt so tall. Her spine felt strong and straight. She looked the squirming girl squarely in the face.

"Listen, girl. Have your fun. He will not marry you. He will go back to the States and leave you here. You'll marry that boy with the lazy eye who you knew from school." Sylvie's face lost its crimson tint and went entirely white. Nathalie gasped and nearly dropped her teacup. Alice gave each of the women a long stare before continuing. "You will have a whole tribe of children.

Your third will fall ill from pneumonia on the day after his fourth birthday, and you'll regret it all your days if you don't get him to the doctor. My husband will tire of you soon, girl, so have your run at it while it lasts. It matters not to me." With that, Alice turned to Beatrice, whose chest was heaving in anger or shock, she could not tell.

"My coat, please. I am leaving."

Beatrice was frozen, and Sylvie was screaming a string of French curses so loudly that even Luc's ears were bent in discontent. Nathalie hurried to the tiny closet and gingerly handed Alice her jacket. With a backward glance, Alice turned the knob to the front door.

"Take the baby to the doctor, girl. Your lazy-eyed husband will tell you not to, and you'll regret it all your days if you listen." With a nod to the stunned Nathalie, Alice swung her coat over her shoulder and stepped out into the English rain that wished to be snow. She could hear the chorus of French curses rise in pitch as Beatrice found her voice. Alice smiled broadly to herself as she strode down the South London street. It wasn't until she stepped off the bus at Miss Lettie's manor house that her bravado gave way and the outrage hit her like a wave. The path shone in front of her as clearly as it had that afternoon on High Street in Glasgow, but now she could see the cracks in the veneer. Paul knew she would meet this Sylvie. This girl was no more dear to him than she was a pawn to hurt Alice. He had used the wretched creature to torment Alice, and once news of this afternoon's tea reached his ears, he would laugh and laugh.

That was the pacing and cursing that Miss Lettie found Alice entrenched in. It wasn't the infidelity; it wasn't the breach of trust or loss. It was the manipulation and the fact that she had played straight into his game. As Alice finished her story, Miss Lettie poured two more cups of tea and added brandy accordingly to both.

"Love, if there's anything I know, it's that men hate to be beaten at their own game. Of course, if you refuse to play, it'll really cheese him off. Your man's blinkered when it comes to love; he doesn't see half of what you are. You want to win this match, you keep on. Not sure about your Jackie O, but the Queen herself would take notice of you in that dress." Miss Lettie reached out and squeezed Alice's hand. Alice found herself sinking back into the stiff couch, the feeling of home all around her, and the inevitability of life left outside in the English rain that wished it were snow.

CATRIONA REID, THE DAUGHTER *of the great Moira Blair, grew up in a rapidly changing world. The expectations that held her mother were largely ignored by this fire-haired girl who grew up half in and half out of the world of spirits. Catriona learned the arts of card reading and how to interpret the future from the lines on the palm of a hand. She read tea leaves and interpreted signs. She knew what it meant when a raven shed its feathers on your steps and how to undo a string of bad luck set about by envious thoughts. Her mother taught her everything she knew, and soon Catriona had her own following of ladies who came to her for teas that would bring love, or herbs to ease depression. The combination of her wild beauty and her mother's money made for a great number of suitors, but married life held no appeal for Catriona. She largely ignored the young men who seemed to hang about her mother's parlor waiting for a chance to hold audience with her. Her interests were far beyond anything they could provide.*

Her mother warned her about spending too much time with the spiritualists of the day. One in particular, a Russian woman transplanted into Britain, was forming a society based on the truth and order of things. They are insulting the spirit realm, her mother told her, her brow furrowed in concern. They do not have the sight, and they take advantage of the fools who do not know better. Catriona ignored the warnings; the Russian woman's teachings were fascinating—dark and filled with poetry and verse from India, the Orient, Tibet. She traveled to London and met the short woman with the azure eyes in person. The woman took Catriona's hand and told her she could see the gift in her; she invited the fire-haired girl to go to New York with her, travel the world—India, Peru—touch the places where the truth and the light were being spread.

Catriona felt intoxicated by the strange, forceful woman who gripped her hand tighter and tighter as she spoke. Stay for a gathering tonight, the Russian woman said; you will see the power of the movement, and you will know it is the right time to leave with us. Catriona drank wine and ate a fine dinner with five of the wealthiest ladies in London that evening. They knew of her mother and were delighted she was to be witness to the séance scheduled in the parlor later that evening. The Lady Lily Campbell had lost her husband to what the doctors told her was consumption and what the gossip circles claimed was syphilis. Her grief was muted, but she was extremely concerned with a strongbox he had mentioned in his will. It was missing, and without it, his not-quite-grieving widow would quickly lose the lifestyle he had afforded her thus far.

Catriona entered the parlor where the dark wood table was lined with candles. Long shadows were cast from the sconces running the length of the room. Something about the scene made Catriona uneasy, but she was merely a guest here, not a participant, so she kept her tongue. The ladies filed in and took their places at the table with soft giggles of anticipation. They waved Catriona into a chair, and all joined hands. It was then that Catriona realized this was a regular occurrence for these women. They were regular guests of the Russian woman, and Lady

Lily's husband was merely the most recent excuse to summon the dead. Catriona realized what was causing her to feel unsettled: this entire thing was a show, a game to them. Her mother's words rolled back and forth in her ears: they are insulting the spirit realm, her mother had said, and they are mocking it.

Just then, with a dramatic throw of the large double doors at the end of the room, the Russian woman entered, a serving man closing the doors behind her and enshrouding the room once again in darkness. The squat, stout woman moved gracefully to a seat at the end of the table. Her hands were adorned with rings, several per finger, giving her the appearance that she was manufactured of disconnected metal bits. Her robes were untidy, they lay in disarray, and the stench of tobacco emanated from every pore of her body. The Russian woman fixed her unearthly blue eyes on the ladies sitting at the table, giving each participant a lengthy, unbroken stare before moving on to the next. When she reached Catriona, she held the gaze longer than with the others. Her face was set, but Catriona swore she saw her mouth lift into a sort of sneer.

Catriona tried to see what had held her earlier, how she had been mesmerized, fixated by this woman. She tried to see the magnetic presence that had captured her and made her want to head immediately to the dock and on to New York. This was false. Catriona could feel the space in the room; there were no spirits, but she doubted very much that the highborn ladies cared at all about that. Their eyes were locked on the Russian woman, and Lady Lily to Catriona's left squeezed her hand as the Russian woman began to speak in a low, rhythmic voice.

"There are two sorts of spirit we will communicate with tonight: the control and the guide. The control is merely here as an intermediary between the spirit world and ours; guides come to us from the upper plane and will return there after they have communicated with us. We must concentrate our energy and thoughts. Watch the candle flames, and keep

your eyes open at all times. The spirits will show you signs, and you must be ready for them."

The sharp sound of the ladies' intake of breath filtered through the room. Catriona's nerves were on end. The Russian woman's gaze was fixed on her, and she could feel her eyes boring into her mind. She knows I know this to be a fraud, Catriona thought; she does not have the gift, but she knows that much. Just then, the Russian woman jerked her head back, and her entire body went stock-still then convulsed forward as though she were being shaken by an unseen force. Despite Catriona's assertion, she jumped with the ladies as the Russian woman's eyes rolled back into her skull and she began muttering unintelligible words. The sounds continued, sometimes forming the corner of a known word or with a cadence that made the gibberish sound conversational. Suddenly, her eyes fixed on Lady Lily, and the muttering ceased.

"My dear." The Russian woman's voice was muted, odd. "My dear," she repeated as Lady Lily gasped. "You've come such a long way. I'm learning ever so much here."

The Russian woman paused as though listening, and then in her familiar, slightly accented English responded, "Hello, you are learning quite a lot aren't you?" She laughed as though someone had told a delightful joke.

Overhead, the chandelier lit with low candlelight began swinging in a slow circle. The ladies jumped, and the Russian woman waved them down. "Relax, my dears. It is only our guide. Mickey is guiding the spirits tonight, aren't you, Mickey?"

In a voice that sounded higher and younger than either of the two they had heard thus far, the Russian woman answered her own question as the ladies around the table quivered and Catriona set to seeking out the corners of the room with her eyes, looking for the tricks she knew must be rigged in this space.

"Yes, Madame. I bring you the departed spirit of Lord Nigel Campbell. He speaks of a message he carries for his wife."

"Nigel?" Lady Lily cried out next to Catriona, squeezing her hand as though to break it.

"My dear." The Russian woman answered in the same muted voice she had used before. "I'm learning ever so much here."

Just then, the overhead chandelier halted its movement, and flashes of light began dancing around the room. One caught Catriona square in the eye, and she was blinded for a split second. The ladies shrieked with delight and fear, and the Russian woman nodded back and forth.

"My dear," the Russian woman continued as Lady Lily began to softly cry.

"Nigel, I'm entirely lost without you," she sobbed theatrically.

Catriona heard the tinkling of tiny bells and remembered what her mother had always told her about the charlatans of her day, the thin wires invisible in a dark space running up a wall and controlled with the medium's foot. Just then the table began to shake, and the women broke their link of hands and ran to the door.

"My dear." The Russian woman intoned. "You will come again, won't you?"

With that, the ladies ran shrieking into the next room, leaving Catriona and the Russian woman alone.

"You're a fraud," Catriona whispered, her voice shaking.

"My dear," the Russian woman said in her natural voice, the corners of her lips curled ever so slightly. "That doesn't matter in the least."

Catriona returned to Glasgow on the next train, the world of the spirits and the energy of all the things her mother had taught her ringing in her ears. She chose a quiet life; the big house on Cathedral Court that her mother had so prized held no interest for her. Most of the young men who hung about lost interest when they saw that Catriona had no interest in the money and estate that would be passed one day from her mother. She was unmarried and entirely scandalous when her own daughter was born. Catriona didn't care a bit about that. She bought a shop with a flat overhead on narrow High Street, where the tenants hung their laundry across the lane. It flapped and fluttered in the Scottish breeze, and Catriona heard the words of the poem by the American writer: a flag of my disposition, he had written. And so it was such.

Catriona settled in this humble place that folded her in as though she had always belonged. She sold herbs to help babies with the grippe and ease heartache. She read palms and cards for those who needed answers. She lived a long life free from illness and full of peace. The vibration of the bloodline rang clear and strong as she taught her daughter the lessons of truth and clarity. And somewhere in the rocky crags, the Cailleach knew that the matriarchal power had been passed and she breathed a sigh that blew as a gentle breeze across the lowland fields.

CHAPTER 27

THE VISION CAME STRONG and fast, nearly knocking Alice off her feet. The woman was lying on a worn wooden table, her cracked climbing helmet still on her head, blood leaking out from the edges. Alice leaned against the banister of the manor house to steady herself, grateful for the ragged antique chair that sat by the foot of the stairs. With her head in her hands, the vision clarified. The woman's skin was already turning greyish, and the blood was pooling beneath her, its source a mystery, as her face looked serene, her body posed in such a manner that she might have just lain down for a nap. That had been done on purpose; Alice could see on the backs of her eyelids the scene play out as though she had been in the room. A man and another woman; the man carried her gently, the woman shaking and crying. They laid her down softly, as though afraid to interrupt her slumber. They knew in their hearts that she was gone, so they left her alone in the hunting cabin to go get help. The woman on the table lay still; she would never move again.

In the vision that played out with a startling degree of clarity, Alice walked around the table, regarding the woman from all angles. She was somewhere in her thirties, maybe forty. Her hair was short and stuck out from under her cracked helmet in sticky tufts. Her slate-grey eyes stared at the ceiling. Faint lines crisscrossed the skin around her eyes; too much sun, too much cold winter air. Her arms and legs were muscular. She was a climber; this was not the result of carelessness or ignorance of the mountain. A freak accident, something had gone wrong, something no one would have seen coming.

Alice could feel breath over her right shoulder. Without even looking, she knew the woman was standing here, staring at her body.

"I don't understand," the woman said softly. "They left me here. Why did they leave?"

Alice turned to face her. The woman's eyes were wide, scared. She wore the tight-fitting activewear and helmet, but there was no blood; her skin held a sun-kissed glow that Alice knew was her natural complexion, not the grey pallor that was steadily overtaking the shell on the table. In a rush of images, Alice saw what had happened: an errant crag of stone falling from above; another climber had left it loose, not knowing what his mistake would cost the next to scale the mountainside. The woman had never even known what had happened. She had reached for the next handhold, her mind focused on the sharpness of the air, the familiar weight of the ropes and harness holding her safely in place. The rock above her had splintered and fallen, killing her instantly. Her friends screamed her name and eventually lowered her body to the ground. Night was falling, and they needed to get help. They'd moved her to the little cabin left here by the forestry service and set out on foot together. No one would return until morning, when the frame on the table would be stiff and pale, the blood congealed around her. It was cold tonight; her husband would worry that she was not back yet. Her friends wouldn't reach a phone until late, long after this woman's loved ones, a man and a small child, would have spent the night calling anyone who might know anything. She would be greatly missed, a hole would be left in her absence. Her spirit, as wild as it was gentle, would not go quietly.

But now this woman stood here in the ice-cold cabin, regarding her own dead body with fear and confusion. Alice reached out and took her hands. They were warm; a force stronger than blood was coursing through her veins now. Soon it would carry her away entirely.

"You died, love," Alice said softly, the twitch of Glasgow from her childhood making its way into her speech. "They didn't abandon you; they went for help."

The woman shifted her gaze to Alice. "Who are you?" she asked, her voice shaking.

"No one of consequence," Alice whispered, and in that moment, she knew exactly why she was here. "It's time to leave this place, love. You're free now, and you can feel it already, yes?" Alice took the woman's other hand and looked into her grey eyes.

The woman nodded. "But they won't know what happened to me . . . . I have to tell them not to worry."

"That's my job, love," Alice said, and the woman gave her a small smile.

"I don't understand how this happened," the woman repeated.

"None of it makes any sense. A loose stone fell and you died. There are worlds within worlds beyond this one, but you have to let go of this place first. Stay too long and you'll find yourself stuck. No need to stay." Alice spoke the words with a certainty whose origin was a mystery.

"Tell them to keep the fire lit; they'll know what it means." The woman took one last look at her steadily greying corpse and turned, walking out the door into the woods. Her form disappeared into night, and in a burst of golden firefly glow, she was gone.

Alice fell forward in the chair, catching herself on the flats of both hands an inch before she would have slammed headfirst into Miss Lettie's wooden floor. She knew immediately what she needed to do. This hadn't happened here. She needed to get the message to her mother. This was something from home, something from the Colorado mountains. The tiny hallway table held a rotary phone. A few operators later, racking up a long-distance bill that would make Miss Lettie grimace, Alice had her mother on the phone. It was the middle of the night there, and Mum's sleep-filled voice was filled with fear and confusion. Yes, she did know what Alice was talking about, as a matter of fact. She'd gotten a call from Caroline Sempsy's husband not an hour ago: she'd gone rock climbing with friends and hadn't returned; none of them had come home yet. The husband was calling everyone in his wife's address book, desperate for a reasonable answer but knowing that something terrible had happened. Alice carefully told Mum about the cabin and the message that the woman with the grey eyes had relayed.

In the weeks to come, Mum would send a letter telling her that the forestry service had found Caroline Sempsy's friends half-frozen to death on the trail. They'd been trying to hike out and had gotten turned around in the dark. Caroline's body was exactly where Alice had said it would be, and her bereaved husband had turned three shades of pale when Mum had told him to keep the fire lit. Mum still didn't know what it meant, but it had definitely meant something of significance. Mum never asked Alice how she had known, although she did get a letter from one of Caroline's friends some time later. It was short and written in neatly printed text, the type of print that one uses when they are trying too hard to maintain control. The woman wanted Alice to know that they hadn't wanted to leave her there, all by herself. She wanted to know if Caroline had blamed her. Alice responded as best she could, but with a flash of the children in that classroom so long ago, and the unconscious men in the street in Caracas, she knew the guilt of the living far outweighs the concerns of the dead.

Any further discussion of the strange incident was soon overshadowed with news of a different sort. The bouts of nausea and dizziness that Alice assumed were a lingering spring cold were diagnosed in a very different manner. She was pregnant, a miracle considering how scarce and scant any intimacy between her and Paul had been. But Alice knew that this baby had been written in the stars long before. She had seen her sweet brown eyes years and years before; she had appeared to her on that lane in Glasgow. This was her daughter who would carry the moon on her shoulders, her daughter whose words would change hearts and minds, her daughter who would feel the ugliness of this world like she was walking on a thousand shards of glass, her daughter who would spend her days half in this world and half in her own head.

As her belly grew steadily rounder, Miss Lettie would pamper her with special teas and meals. Paul would never speak of Sylvie again, would promise that this was the change they both needed. Alice would believe him for a time, and later on still, as she watched him with their infant daughter in Miss Lettie's ancient rocking chair, singing her songs of spiders and flies, she would see the pain and sadness lift, and the promise that had danced in the mist back on that lane in Glasgow would seem somehow possible.

CHAPTER 28

THE LITTLE SHOP ON *the lane was well-known throughout Glasgow. Some knew of it by association: the daughter of the great Moira Blair ran it and lived in the flat overhead with her own daughter, who had the trademark fiery hair and dark eyes of her mother and grandmother. Some knew it for Catriona, herself, and her indelible ability to know all that was troubling you without ever hearing a word. Some knew it for the strange stories that swirled around the daughter, who was swiftly becoming a woman. Muriel had been named for a many-greats grandmother around whom swirled stories of ancient witchery and a mysterious cult of powerful women. There was no saying if the stories were true, but Catriona had hoped that her daughter would find strength in her family name and not be swayed by frauds as she herself had been once.*

It was a difficult time. The séances and spiritualism that the Russian woman claimed to hold power over had become overwhelmingly popular, especially among the wealthy women of Edinburgh and London. Glasgow held a more working-class sort of sensibility, and as such, Catriona's shop was publicly an entirely unmagical apothecary, as held with the ancient and outdated witchcraft laws. However, anyone who paid the least bit of attention knew its real intent. The authorities looked the other way, and a wary peace held. Catriona was approached frequently, as many had heard of her one-time association with the Russian woman, and even though the Russian had been proven a fraud long ago, her philosophy lived on and her followers were seemingly everywhere.

Muriel was a curious girl; she took to the herbal mixtures and teas her mother taught her easily. She grew a line of herbs in her bedroom window and collected flowers from the fields outside of town. The teenager seemed to have little to no interest in others her age, and even though she attended the newly formed higher primary school and was subject to all manner of compulsory social interaction, she always seemed to exist in her own world.

For her part, Muriel did not much see the point of the higher primary school. She had learned to read from her mother at a very young age and had from that point on read everything put in front of her. She learned of wars and queens and kings. She learned geometry and higher math and philosophy. She lost herself in the sordid and gory stories of the saints and martyrs and learned the Latin names of plants and animals from the crumbling books in her grandmother Moira's library. But her real education was spent on the heath. As soon as she could slip away and change the stiff, scratchy school uniform for soft cotton, she headed to the fields that surrounded the city. It was here she discovered that by sitting very still under the great rowan tree by the edge of the woods and emptying her head, she could call the butterflies to land on her shoulders and hands. She discovered that storm clouds manifested when she was in a foul mood and cleared as she unwound her unhappiness.

She knew the neighbors whispered about her and sometimes appeared in the shop with gawking eyes and shy questions. A young woman once approached Muriel as she ground peppermint and wormwood at the shop's work table, and in a tumble of words explained that she was getting married on Saturday next and could Muriel maybe make her a charm to keep the rain at bay and storm clouds clear. Muriel had kindly explained that it doesn't quite work that way, but at the teary eyes of the young woman, she mixed a small bag of allspice, cinnamon, and mint. The woman thanked her profusely and overpaid for the simple mixture by far. Muriel didn't guarantee a rain-free day, but at the very least the mixture would smell pleasant and bring luck to whomever kept it close.

It was on the day of the wedding when the storm broke. It started as a rain-free and entirely cloudless day. Muriel was pleased that the bride with her bag of sweet-smelling herbs wouldn't have to suffer the weather and was more pleased that she wouldn't have to hear about it later on when said bride came to complain. As she walked through the field toward the shelter of a large rowan tree, she spied movement from the base on the soft mossy ground. Startled, Muriel stopped and observed. A boy a bit older than she was leaning up against the trunk as though he were waiting. She had never seen anyone out in the fields the way she was; there were others, of course, the farmers who made their way back and forth to the city, and the children who rolled and played in the rough grass. But Muriel was typically the only one content to spend hours sitting under a tree or get lost in her head collecting wildflowers and the herbs that grew at the edge of the woods. But here was another, and in the spot that she frequented most. Suddenly she began to feel the electricity in the air prickling at her fingertips.

Muriel turned to leave, her skin tingling in warning. As she moved, the boy heard the rustle in the rough grass and stood. He was tall, taller than she'd thought, and older. He grinned, but even from a bit of a distance Muriel could see that it was the sort of smile that lived on his lips only, a smile meant to fool others. He waved and took a step forward.

Muriel regarded him for a moment, spun, and headed back to the city gate. She heard footsteps moving faster behind her, catching up to her quickly. All the hairs on her back and neck on end, Muriel quickly weighed her options. To her left, the forest was closer than the city gate. She knew the forest as well as she knew her own home; there were a dozen places to hide where no one would ever find her. If she ran to the gates to the right, she risked being overtaken, and on this fair, cloudless day, no one was around to see what was happening.

Ice traveled up Muriel's back into her heart. More footsteps sounded behind her. Dreading the sight, she swiveled as she ran and saw three other boys—no, not boys, men—in step with the first. Where had they come from, she wondered silently. They must have been hiding by the edge of the woods, waiting for the first to make a move. What did they want? She broke into a run as she heard the steps behind her quickening their pace. A pelt of laughter broke from behind her.

"C'mon, little witch!" they jeered. "We only want to talk to ya."

Muriel judged the distance to the city gates; no one was around, no one could hear her scream or cry out. The woods to her left were closer; she could make it to the woods, and once there she could lead them to where hunters laid their sharp-clawed traps. She knew the spot well, as usually she went and sprung them when no one was about; today, though, she knew they were set, and with a bit of misdirection, the men who were still calling after her and pacing into a run themselves would be caught in the mire of blades and snapping jaws. With a breath, she steeled her will and veered to the left, the alder and elm trees greeting her into their secluded darkness.

"Little witch!" the men called after her. "Little witch, are you hiding?"

Muriel dodged the ancient trunks and waited to see if they would follow. She knew the path that would take them to the traps. Her question was answered with the snapping of branches and leaves as the men entered the woods after her.

"You know witching's a crime, don't you?" a voice called, an edge to the words. "We're only here to warn you what happens to abominations like yourself."

Muriel ducked and ran down the familiar path, the footsteps behind her gaining speed. Of course they know the woods, she thought wildly. They might even be the ones who set the traps. Still she blundered on, the voices behind her getting louder and louder.

"Clever girl. We know where you're leading us. You don't really think we'll go traipsing through our own traps, now, do ya?"

Muriel stopped. Her chest heaving, she ducked behind the trunk of a giant elm, hoping the undergrowth and ferns were enough to mask her. The footsteps steadily approached. The men were laughing.

"We're not tryin' to fleg you, little one, but we think that maybe no one's told you that witchin's a crime. You know what they did to witches back in the day?"

Muriel was shaking, her breath ragged. The crunch of the leaves and bramble came closer, closer, closer. All of a sudden, she had a clear picture in her head of the man who had been sitting under the tree. He had been at her mother's shop several weeks back, staring in the window. Mum had shivered as though suddenly chilled and stared him back down until he moved and walked down the street. She hadn't spoken of it then or since, and Muriel had not seen the man again until today.

"It's the devil's work, little witch." A voice boomed so close that Muriel had to stifle a scream. "We know all about your mother and grandmother, and they might have charmed the authorities, but God doesn't give a feck about all that."

The crunching of leaves and twigs stopped, and Muriel held her breath. Then she felt a sharp stab of pain as her head was yanked backward by the hair and she was dragged out from behind the elm. A scream that sailed through the treetops escaped her lips, but the men only laughed.

"C'mon, little witch, none of that."

A length of stinking cloth was stuffed in her mouth as two of the laughing men pinned down her arms and legs to the forest floor. Muriel could hear the crack of storm clouds overhead and feel the rain that had burst from the sky filtering through the trees. Lightning streaked across the sky, and the rowan tree burst into flames.

"What'd we tell you about witchin'?" the smiling man asked as he undid his belt.

Far off in the lowland crags, the black water of the underground lake stirred and sent cascading ripples to lap the rocky shore. The Cailleach awakened with a start. A storm was raging, and the stifled screams of her many-greats granddaughter filled her ears. With a cry that shook the walls of the cave and sent a ripple across the rough grass of the heath, the Cailleach lurched to the entrance of her cave, her movements savage and deliberate. The air hit her withered skin for the first time in a thousand years. She raised her arms to the sky and summoned the wind and rain; she felt in the darkness for the hidden terrors, those that had lain dormant alongside her for a thousand long years. Many miles away, the men were knocked from their feet by a blast of arctic air, bits of ice and hail like razors cutting into their skin, piercing their eyes and blinding them. They screamed in pain and surprise. Lightning shot from the sky, splintering the elm and sending dancing bits of flame to light among the forest. The men were reduced to a series of parts, all their ugliness and hate now a severed leg or bodiless elbow, a bit of an ear and a tangle of intestine. The ensuing fire would consume most, and what was left went to the badgers and wildcats.

Muriel crawled from the blaze through the storm of ice and rain, her body aching and bloody. She had no tears left and instead was filled with a rage that overtook her entirely. Raising herself to all fours, she placed her hands on the ground and channeled all the horror in her body and mind into the earth. The ley lines quivered and shook, channeling the curse under the earth and straight under the city walls. In that moment, Muriel had no regard for anyone; no one was innocent. They came to her for herbs, and then they descried her for a witch. She fell back shaking as the rain subsided and the fire simmered to a low burn. The curse sent by the many-greats granddaughter of Cailleach crept into the shadows and alleyways of Glasgow; it infected the water and caught the twilight breeze, blowing into the windows of the young and old alike.

The first fell ill almost immediately, coughing to raise the blood from the lungs. Hundred upon hundreds followed. They died slowly, their own lungs deteriorating bit by bit, their bodies wracked with pain and terror. The curse did not discriminate, and the young died alongside the grown ones. As the forest still burned, as the curse was being spread and the first of so many fell ill, the Cailleach lurched back to her nest by the shores of the black lake, deep within her cave, and folded back into herself. She felt the vibration of the ley lines and the power of the young hag. She also felt the inevitability of what was to come.

The child was born nine months to the date of the great storm. The curse still swirled around the city, and no one understood why Muriel or her mother seemed unconcerned about the baby catching the consumption that was killing so many. Both Muriel and Catriona knew this child was immune to such human blights, evil as her conception was. The line of hags from which she descended assured that she was to be extraordinary. She was named Rowan, after the patch of beauty and comfort on the fields that had been destroyed forever. The hags of Glasgow closed around her and taught her the secrets of their kind, and the Cailleach settled back into her sleep deep within the lowland crags.

CHAPTER 29

COIRA ANNE COSLET. Alice was filling out the paperwork that would create a birth certificate and eventually a passport for the tiny, perfect creature that was currently sleeping in her cot. Born on the longest night of the year, when the new- shorn summer had not yet begun to warm in the English sun. Paul hadn't understood why Alice was so set on the name; he had wanted to look at the baby book, and he had suggested Karen or maybe Susan. Alice had turned him down flat. There was a slew of family names to choose from, and Alice had carefully considered the long line of women from whence she had come. She nearly decided upon Catherine, or even the older spelling, Catriona, but ultimately decided upon a name she had found scrawled into the pages of the family Bible, a many-times ancient grandmother. Alice liked the sound of it, the smooth sea rocks that washed up on the Scottish shore. Paul had been baffled. In his family, names were chosen because they sounded nice; not nearly so much consideration to the history of the name was given. Alice knew better: names held power. It would be up to the wee little baby with the pink cheeks and honey-fire eyes to pass on another carefully chosen family name.

"What if it'd been a boy?" Paul had asked, his face scrunched up in bafflement as he slowly accepted the way things would be.

"Then he would be Arthur after my brother, but that would change nothing. The tradition follows the first-born daughter; she will inherit all the things from the old country." Alice tried to be patient. Paul had shaken his head, not understanding. His family might still have a foothold in their old Welsh ways, but they had been in the states far longer than Alice's. They had forgotten the power of names and tradition.

In her cot, Coira started to fuss, and Alice looked up, startled. She was due for a nappy change. The fresh ones were still on the line at the back of the house. A service stopped by every other day, but they never seemed to keep up with the demand. They left a stack of fresh cloth squares, and they'd cart the dirty away. But Alice felt bad sending them with the stink and mess, so she washed them in the utility sink out back and hung them up on the line, her baby in a basket next to her in the grassy yard, cooing at the ivory flags flying in the English breeze. Alice had taken a semi-permanent leave from the International School. They'd offered her a full year's leave, but she hadn't made any indication that she intended to return. They seemed somewhat unconcerned.

Mum and Polly were due the week after next; they were all going to take a train up to Glasgow with Coira, see the old house in Cathedral Court that still belonged to their line and had a caretaker hired by Mum. The girl's school that had occupied its halls for so long had closed years ago, and now the caretaker, with Mum's blessing, rented out the rooms to boarders. The little stone cottage far on the end of the land surrounding the manor house, where Grandmum Rowan and Granddad had lived, where they had sought shelter during the war, still stood, housing the caretaker. The little shop on High Street that Alice held so dear to her childhood was now a bakery and teashop. Alice tingled with excitement at the thought of the trip. Her memories of her childhood were fragmented, a bit from the country house, a bit from High Street. Alice's heart ached when she thought of Gran; she remembered her long, silver braid curling over her shoulder and her tea that tasted slightly of vanilla. She'd been six the last time she'd seen her in the flesh, but that hadn't been goodbye. Alice never told Mum, but Gran had visited her nearly every night since her passing.

She'd been in Caracas when Gran had passed. Alice had known immediately. She was teaching, in the middle of a lesson, and a wave had hit her. She stepped back and steadied herself on the chalkboard, smearing the notes her students were struggling to copy down. There was no explaining how she knew; it was as though a piece of her had been ripped away—a lung, a heart, a bit of her very soul. Tears were already streaming down her cheeks when she ran out of the room and to the front desk clerk. They assumed that she had received a phone call, or the grief was just sneaking up on her. No one had questioned her when she ran home to the tiny apartment she shared with Lupe. She was met by her neighbor, an older man who smoked pungent cigars and often brought over bottles of rum to share. "You have a visitor," he had said. "I would have been happy to entertain her if I'd known." Alice had shaken her head, and the man had looked confused. "She was right out on your balcony earlier.

Nice looking lady—your grandmother? Dressed a bit warm for the weather."

Alice had shaken her well-meaning neighbor off and found herself on the balcony, her entire body aching with the loss. It had been Gran on the balcony; Alice could see her clear as day now, standing tall with her black knit sweater and long skirt. Her silver braid, an entity in itself, catching the dying sun. She had come to say goodbye, and never again would Alice hear her scratchy voice over the phone or read a new letter in her hawkish script.

But soon enough, Alice would be able to set wildflowers at the gravesite where she lay with others of her line in the Necropolis, and walk down the lane where she had so long ago played as a child. Her own infant Coira would look at the same sky that her namesake had, and it all seemed as though it were coming full circle. None of the rest of it mattered. The pain it had taken to get her here was washed away. Alice crossed to the fussy baby and lifted her in her arms, singing softly to her.

Through the world I am wandering, wandering
These are the days I live now
Through the world I am wandering, wandering
A soft breeze blowing

In these soft moments time stopped, and Alice knew that the planets were aligning at last. The vision she had been given so many years ago back on the lane in Glasgow was slipping into sync, and the world was falling into place at long last.

CHAPTER 30

IN THIS WAY TIME passed, and Coira grew from infant to toddler to little girl. She was stoic and serious, her honey-fire eyes taking in everything that went on around her. Life went on as it did. Great stretches of time passed before Paul would turn up at Miss Lettie's, but he always brought books and toys for Coira. The pair of them would sit together while Paul sang the little girl songs from a crumbling book of nursery rhymes.

There was an old lady who swallowed a fly
I don't know why she swallowed a fly
I guess she'll die

The child, barely out of toddlerhood, would listen as though she were being read a legal document: she studied the words and offered no smile or giggle as a sign of approval. Alice watched the two of them and saw a flash of why she had forgiven Paul so very much: he was patient and kind, and never once did he question why the little girl was unlike others of her age. She's smarter than most everyone else, he said once after Coira had fallen asleep and they'd gently placed her in the cot in Alice's room. Alice had just nodded. She was smarter than the lot of those around her, and everything that happened was absorbed in her honey-fire eyes and processed silently behind her unreadable face.

Time passed. Miss Lettie watched the little girl as Alice went back to teaching. She said she felt as though she were a grand-mum again. Alice felt she could continue this life forever if it were granted, but it was not to be. She had seen a great many things on that day as a child on High Street, and she knew that the path that had been laid out so many years ago would come to pass. She shivered at the images that had been shown to her, some clear and some nonsensical and chilling.

And so when Paul told Alice that he was leaving for the States in seven days, Alice was not surprised. She was not quite sure as to exactly what had prompted the swift departure, and Paul was not telling. Alice did get a bit of a hint at the truth of the situation from one of the other wives who lived on the base, a stout, mannish sort of woman named Corinne who ran the monthly spouse dinners on the base. Alice didn't always attend, but since Coira's arrival, she had been a more regular guest. The dinner had fallen the night after Paul had broken the news to Alice. It was a paperwork thing, he had said, a transfer. It had to do with his hearing loss; he couldn't do the work, so he was being transferred back to Colorado Springs to a desk job. Alice hadn't quite believed him, but they were at a place where the truth was negotiable. This was a more savory version of the truth, and the effort Paul had put into concocting the story was rather sweet.

Coira had the run of Miss Lettie's house now. "Far too young to be so independent," the old woman had sighed. Alice had no comparison; she thought Coira to be right on schedule. The determined little girl had been set in her own ways from the very beginning. At barely a year, she had even managed the great wooden stairs. Her brow would furrow, and she would gently and purposefully edge her way down. Alice had held her breath the entire first time she'd done it, but now it was a regular sight.

Paul's face had frozen a bit when Alice told him that she wasn't following him back home. He hadn't said anything for a few sullen moments, but swallowed hard, and then, in a carefully measured tone, he asked, "What will you do for money? I don't intend to send money back for you to stay here."

Alice had laughed—a most inappropriate response, but entirely spontaneous. She hadn't relied on Paul's meager contributions to her living expenses since the first few months of her arrival.

"Have you forgotten that I have a job, and that I was born in this country?" Alice had said airily. It was true: she had maintained dual citizenship since childhood, and her job paid well enough for her to live in Miss Lettie's house forever if she chose to.

Paul had left for the base, and Alice had sat with Miss Lettie in the drawing room, drinking brandy-spiked tea while Coira drew pictures with her charcoal pencils by the fireplace. You're a brave one, Miss Lettie had said. Alice had shaken her head. She was far from brave; she was a coward, all things considered. She knew what lay in the path for Paul, and there was nothing she could do to change his stars. She had her baby, and as far as she considered things, it was all she needed. She liked England with its sprawling moors, and this house with its drafty windows felt like home.

So Alice had gone to what she supposed would be her last spouse dinner at Corinne's dreadful grey concrete flat on the base. All the wives were supposed to bring a dish, and Alice had brought a pot of her grandmother's chicken noodles, which swiftly disappeared among the gelatin molds and potato casseroles. Corinne had pulled Alice aside while Coira sat with a little boy of similar size, not playing as he was exactly, but observing, as was her way. Alice watched the little boy sorting through a bucket of Lincoln Logs by the foot of the stairs, absorbed in the activity. Alice smiled at her little girl's furrowed brow as she watched the boy build a house from the bits of wood.

"I wanted to know how you're holding up, love?" Corinne had asked.

Alice gave a polite smile. "It will be a big change, but Paul's hearing has been shot since Vietnam, so I suppose it's not too big a surprise." There was no need to tell anyone her plans to stay in the UK. It was none of their business, after all, and the chances of any of the base wives finding out she had stayed behind were slim.

Corinne had frowned. "So you really don't know, then."

Alice had, of course, known there was much more to the story than Paul had told her, and she supposed this moment was inevitable.

"I'm quite frankly not sure I want to know," she said simply.

Corinne took this as an invitation to tell the whole story in hushed tones while Alice watched her little girl stack blocks across the room. Paul was being sent home not because his hearing had impaired his ability to do his job, but because he had had a breakdown in his commander's office. Corinne didn't know all the details; her husband was a clerk and had heard from someone who had seen it happen through the glassed walls of the office. Paul had nearly broken his hand hammering it through the glass. The commander had ordered a psychiatric evaluation and a transfer back home. It wasn't unheard of, Corinne whispered, nothing to be ashamed of; the men who had seen combat in Vietnam had issues that others simply could not appreciate. She told the entire story in sympathetic murmurings that held an edge of delight at being the one to break such gossip.

Alice had simply nodded her head and walked across the room to Coira, who looked up at her mother with her dark eyes.

"Hello," the little girl said simply.

Alice smiled as she held out her hand, and Coira stood to take it as the other hens in the room whispered mundane sympathies to each other. Poor dear, and what would I do if, and whatnot of the sort. Alice ignored it all; she had the ability to floor them all if she wanted. It was tempting as all hell to tell gossipy Corinne that her husband would fail to come home in about three years, after she had added a red-nosed little boy to their growing brood of children. She would panic and fuss and then get a note written on the back of a postcard saying he was sorry. The husband and father of the red-nosed brood of young ones would be living in Malta at that time, AWOL from the Air Force and entirely in love with a girl who was the polar opposite of Corinne.

It was no use to tell her, and no one would believe her if she did. Looking around the room, the noise seemed to hum; the paths of these women, who had focused their entire beings on waiting for a sense of forever, were laid clearly before her eyes. She closed her eyes and tried to block the rush of lives not her own. She had known that Paul hadn't told her the truth, and she wasn't surprised in the least at Corinne's story. She simply wanted all the sad looks to stop being directed her way. She was okay, she had her place at last in this world, and Paul's indiscretions, his instability, didn't reflect on her in the least. A hushed giggle escaped from a set of lips. Alice could not place the source, but the eyes of the gossipy hens settled on her, waiting for her to react. An old anger, one that Alice had not listened to for quite some time, stirred within her.

"My dear, maybe it's time you went," Corinne said, taking note of the stares and subdued whispers.

Alice nodded, and with a flick of her wrist sent a salad bowl sitting on the edge of the buffet table flying across the room. The women screamed and ducked. Alice smiled sublimely.

"You're right. I do need to be getting on," she said, and with another flick of the wrist overturned a platter of Cornish pasties. Alice didn't wait for a response. She turned and found Coira standing at her heel, a small smile on her face at the chaos, holding her stuffed bear and jumper, ready to go.

As they walked down the steps of the base cottage, Alice laughed aloud at the women's reactions. They would blame it on the wind or perhaps a misplaced hand, and always be fearful of Alice for reasons they couldn't quite name. As for Paul, Alice steeled herself. She was sad for Coira, who loved her Daddy, and watching the two of them read together at bedtime made her love Paul a bit, but Coira was young and would find joy in so many other things and people.

Later at Miss Lettie's, as Coira lay asleep in her cot and Alice lay on the great, dark oak bed staring out the window, she smiled to herself. Her life could really begin now—no expectations, no waiting for the fate she had seen so long ago. Paul would be gone this time next week, and Alice would be free. Maybe she could go back to Glasgow and find a teaching position, or maybe run a shop like her Great-Grandmum Muriel. She could live in the same lane where she'd grown up. Coira could play in the Scottish rain and grow up without the constraints of seeing the paths and intents of all those around her. Alice would let fate play out around her, time and life enough as it was. The path that Alice had seen so many years ago was still intact, and she knew it was unlikely they could escape it altogether, but it was a beautiful dream, and in this night, as the stars filled the English sky and danced in the rolling heath, it was real enough.

CHAPTER 31

ROWAN ELIZABETH REID LEANED *up against the stained and battered wall of the surgery ward in Royaumont Abbey. The young man inside had been on the table for six hours and lost both legs, and it would be a miracle if he lasted the night.*

Rowan was a nurse, for now, studying under the senior doctors. Miss Frances Ivens herself had told her that after the war, she would see that she was accepted to the finest medical school in all of Britain. But for now she assisted and learned whatever any of the doctors and senior nurses were willing to teach. Her mother and grandmother had been wary when she had joined the ranks of the Scottish Women's Hospital. She'd only just finished the preliminary medical training at Queen Margaret's when she'd attended a talk held by Dr. Sybil Lewis, who had implored the scant number of young women at the Women's Medical College to join, to be part of the future of the suffrage movement. Think of it, she'd said to Mum and Grandmum. Think of it, women doctors, nurses, everything. Her Mum had hmph'd and nodded. Sure, she'd said, and what thanks will ya get? You think the soldiers will let a woman save them and not extract their bit of blood for it? Mum hadn't been entirely off; the idea had been met with a great deal of resistance, but now the SWH was stationed all along the front. Rowan had kissed Mum, Grandmum, and Great-Grandmum Moira goodbye and left for France that same year.

Some of the other girls knew about Rowan's family. They knew about her Great-Grandmum Moira, who, even in the furthest reaches of old age, attracted followers and those who wanted her to contact their lost husbands, their children who had died of influenza or consumption. They knew the stories about her Grandmum Catriona and even her mother, who hardly left the flat or the shop below. Some of the other girls teased her, asked her to read their palms or tea leaves. Rowan laughed back, and in an easy way, the scrutiny was lost to the chaos of the hospital. Truth was, Rowan had never much taken to the reading of palms or tea leaves. She didn't have the ability to talk to the spirits that her Great-Grandmum Moira or Grandmum Catriona did. She couldn't call the rain or mix herbs that brought fertility or luck like her Mum. No, Rowan, despite diligent studies with the three great women of her family, was a bit hopeless. She buried her head in science and books. In her secondary studies, she was the only girl in her anatomy class; she had driven the professor mad with questions and angered the boys by scoring higher than any of them. She was fluent in the languages of chemistry and biology to such an extent that she often forgot how to normalize her conversations for regular folk. Mum's eyes would glaze over as she listened, and Rowan would know that she had lost her attention.

The war needed nurses, and Rowan had seen it as a way to achieve her goal. One day she would be a doctor, one of a small but growing club of women physicians in Britain like Dr. Elsie Inglis or Dr. Mary Phillips. Today she had assisted the anesthesiologist and kept the young man breathing and unconscious. The ether was strong, and too much would kill him as easily as the wounds to his legs. Her starched white uniform was stained with blood, and her feet ached as if they would fall straight off. She needed to change and get back to the ward. She was on duty tonight and would be looking in on the young man who would never walk again but might open his eyes nonetheless. Another nurse passed her and offered a weary smile. Rowan returned it. She forced herself to move and walk down the hall to the dormitories, where she could change her clothes and maybe catch a bit of rest before her next shift began.

The young man had bright blue eyes, the color of robin's eggs in summer, and hair that was just a shade off the dark fire-red that ran in her family. He had looked up at her as the ether began to take effect and locked his eyes on hers. Rowan had squeezed his hand and checked the meter to make sure the drip was steady. He couldn't be any older than she, and yet his path had already been decided for him in so many ways. He would most likely die; injuries as grievous as his were likely to catch infection, and even if they didn't, he would be susceptible to the influenza and chest ailments that swirled around the abbey like a storm. Still, she couldn't get his robin's egg eyes out of her mind as she stripped off the stained uniform and donned another, lay back on her cot, and closed her eyes, careful not to let herself get too comfortable.

He took a fever in the night, and Rowan joined the small circle of nurses at the foot of his bed. He thrashed back and forth, pouring sweat, face red and tormented. The doctor, a tiny woman from Liverpool, shooed them all away.

"Go on, girls, let's get back to work. You—I can use you. You stay." She pointed to Rowan.

So Rowan sat by the bedside of the blue-eyed soldier most of the night, helping the doctor give the man fluids through an IV in his arm and wiping his brow. She talked to him, told him stories about her mother and Grandmum, sang him bits of songs that had been sung to her.

Oh do you remember a long time ago
Two poor little babes whose names I don't know
Were stolen away one bright summer day
And left in the woods, So I've heard people say

He moaned and sometimes made sounds that resembled words. At one point, he opened both eyes and again locked them on Rowan.

"I left the gate open, the goats will be loose." His voice sounded young, like a little boy. Rowan took his hand and wiped his brow, and he settled back, shaking slightly. Rowan sang softly to him.

And when it was night
So bleak was their plight
The sun went down
The moon gave no light

He never spoke again or even opened his eyes. He lay still, and Rowan was filled with a concrete certainty that his spirit had flown. She wiped his brow once more and patted down his mussed hair. She wished she had the sight; she wished she could speak to his spirit now and tell him she was sorry she couldn't do more. The young man with the blue eyes died just before dawn.

The next day, the tiny doctor from Liverpool led Rowan to the back of the abbey where there had once stood a great greenhouse.

"The girls tell me that you have knowledge of herbs and plants. Is this true?" she asked pointedly.

"Yes, ma'am. My mother and grandmother…" Rowan answered softly.

"I know who your family is, Nurse Reid. I'm not one to buy into all that. But you have grown up with a knowledge of plants, true?" The doctor's voice was stern but not unkind.

Rowan nodded, and so she became the head of the greenhouse and medicinal herb room. She grew garlic and cinnamon for fever, wormwood and peppermint for dysentery, valerian and St John's wort for pain. She taught the others how to grind the leaves and roots, how to make teas and poultices, how to reduce a bruise with witch hazel and chamomile, how to ease the blindness that came from shock with gingko and bilberry. She felt herself easing back into her childhood, and she knew the women waiting for her in Glasgow would be proud.

Many years later, after the war, after she had completed her studies at Queen Margaret Medical College for Women, where Dr. Frances Ivens, true to her word, had recommended Rowan with highest honors for the work she had done at Royaumont Abbey, Rowan still saw the soldier with the robin's egg blue eyes in her dreams. His face persisted, and his little-boy voice hung in her ears. She sang the little song to her own daughter and prayed she would fear neither death nor the power of her own mind. Rowan Elizabeth Reid lived a long life, free of illness and full of peace, and deep in the lowland crags the Cailleach lay curled in her nest by the black waters in deep hibernation.

CHAPTER 32

THE FLIGHT TO NEW YORK was just under eight hours, and then it would be another seven to Colorado. Eight hours for Alice to sit, with Coira alternately in her lap or wiggling in the seat next to her. Eight hours to close her eyes and smell the sweet Ceylon black tea that Miss Lettie would be brewing right about now. Eight hours to close her eyes and take a mental walk through the little flat in Glasgow that she had signed lease papers for. One bedroom and a den that was perfectly adaptable for a child's bedroom. It smelled of cedar and warm things, and Alice had known as soon as she stepped over the entry that it was hers. The manager had been very understanding, refunding her entire deposit.

"It's a good thing, it is," he had said in a thick brogue. "To be with family in such a time as this." He had nodded at Coira, who was running her hand along the wall, singing quietly to herself, a tune of gibberish that wasn't intended for adult ears. Alice had nodded, her disappointment and grief at the loss of her potential life still bitter and sharp. Out back of the flat was a tiny garden surrounded by a tall and ancient wall. Alice had closed her eyes and seen it lined with garden boxes and a tea table with a couple of chairs. She had seen it filled with snow in the winter and green and balmy in the summer. So as she handed the keys back to manager with his paternal smile, she said a silent goodbye to these visions.

Eight hours to remember every detail. Eight hours to feel Miss Lettie's arms around her shoulders. Eight long hours. Coira, true to her nature, never fussed—or spoke at all, for that matter. She hadn't spoken any more than was necessary since the incident. When a stewardess offered her a cookie with a broad smile, she was notably disconcerted when Coira responded with little more than a solemn nod. They ate a dry chicken dinner, Coira methodically cutting hers into precisely sized cubes of meat before she would take a single bite. Eight hours to sip the weak tea and wish it had a bit of Miss Lettie's brandy in it.

Paul had been gone a bit over a month when she found out. She had signed for the flat in Glasgow and was packing her and Coira's things into a suitcase and a set of milk crates. It was amusing how few possessions they actually had. The furniture was, of course, Miss Lettie's, and Alice had never cared much for fancy clothes or shoes. She had reached up to clear off the top of the bureau, and a wave of milky fog had enveloped her. The last thing she remembered was the freedom of the fall: all responsibility to move her body or prevent the inevitable vanished. She had awoken to Coira and Miss Lettie standing over her and looming down on her like a pair of gargoyles. Miss Lettie had brought her an ice pack for the steadily increasing lump on the back of her head and a cup of tea to fix everything else.

Miss Lettie had looked at Alice with a crookedly furrowed brow.

Alice knew what Miss Lettie suspected, but it was not the stirring of a new life in her belly that had caused her to faint. This was of a much darker nature. A vision had filled Alice's eyes and clouded everything else. It was unclear, but as soon as she found her feet, she had run to the phone in the hall and called Mum, the one person who would need no context to her question.

As she suspected, Mum had promised to call her back and set to investigating. Miss Lettie brought Alice a cold cloth for her head and brought Coira a tea and biscuit, which she happily accepted. The little girl was currently pawing through a book full of photographs of dogs of the Windsors and smiling at a black-and-white photo of a young Elizabeth II kissing a corgi. Between the uncommunicative nature of Paul's family and the time difference, Alice would have to wait a full twelve hours to find out what had knocked her to the floor.

The story relayed to her so many hours later started with Mum calling Paul's mother and sister to find out where he had been staying since he'd returned to Colorado Springs. They had told her to bugger off and hung up. Three times they had told her that, and it was only on the fourth call that they relented. What business of it was hers, they had sneered. "Your darling daughter has gone off and left him. What does she want to do, come crawling back now?" It was only after a series of distinctly Scottish curses that didn't need threats to bolster them that Paul's Welsh mother had given Mum an address.

"You think the polis in Glasgow were bad?" Mum had said with disdain. The local sheriff saw no reason to go knocking on a man's door when he hadn't done anything wrong and there was no call to believe he was in any danger. Mum had eventually driven to the little basement apartment herself. It was a miserable structure, tucked under a dilapidated cabin, devoid of light and looking more hole than house. He hadn't answered the door, and Mum had gone to the family upstairs, from whom Paul rented the basement. They saw no cause for worry; he was a homebody, very quiet. But it had become clear that the old woman wasn't budging, so they had found a key and walked to the rusted metal door to let her in.

Mum strictly refused to describe what she saw in the wretched apartment, but Alice did not need the words. She could see it in her mind's eye. The kitchen sink overflowed with filthy dishes and bits of rotted food; flies swarmed at the destruction. The refrigerator door hung open; the smell of sour milk hung in the air. The landlords grew immediately panicked and ran upstairs to call 911. Mum had walked on into the apartment, past the shag-carpeted living area furnished with milk crates and a folding chair and into a hallway that reeked of rot. There was no light, and all Mum could see was the faint outline of the water pipes that lined the ceiling. The bathroom stood at the end of the hall, the door slightly open, and Mum had walked on, holding her breath so as not to let the gorge rise within her.

He had been floating in the foul water for days, the doctors later said. Mum had no knowledge of how they determined that; his skin was sucked back from his face, his rust-colored hair the only glimmer of color on his grey and pallid corpse. The walls were covered in symbols that meant nothing to anyone but the wretched figure in the tub. Painted with blood, some were pictures, some were words in a language that didn't exist as far as Mum could tell. It made no sense. She stood there, bearing witness to the end he had brought on himself, the empty pill bottles lining the floor around him, a cobweb crust of sticky white over his mouth and eyes.

There was no note, no apparent reason for such a tragedy. Alice had listened as Mum talked, her voice stoic and pragmatic. "You should know that it's the belief on his side that all this was because of you staying back. It's hogwash, of course. You know that—it's utter hogwash. There was a demon in that young man that no one could have protected him against; it's been waiting to come out since he was born to this world, and he lost the fight is all. You don't listen to the rubbish they're saying."

Alice had nodded as though her Mum could see and accepted what it was she had to do. Her daughter needed to say goodbye to her father, she needed to settle his affairs in the States, and she needed to decide her next move. She needed her mum and aunt, and it would take time. Keeping the rent on the flat in Glasgow was more than she could afford to do from the States, and Alice had no earthly idea how long it would take to close out the chapter of her life with Paul. So she said goodbye to the little flat on Bell Street, not far from her childhood home and a long walk to her Many-Greats Grandmum Moira's grand house. She said goodbye to Miss Lettie and the magical room at the top of the stairs. She packed their things and said goodbye and bought plane tickets to a country she'd sworn she'd never return to. "You'll be back, love," Miss Lettie had whispered in her ear as they hugged one last time. Alice had nodded silently. She would, she had no doubt, but her eyes and throat still burned. She would have to start over once again when she returned, and at that moment, the task seemed overwhelming.

Mum called the night before the flight and told her that they had found a note of sorts, not anything that explained but something she felt was meant for Alice nonetheless. "Read it," said Alice, and Mum had paused, then recited with a hint of the old country in her voice.

"Your hat flew from a trash truck and nearly drove me off the road when I was seventeen, and I've known from that moment on that you would be in my life forever. I'm not one to believe in coincidences, and luck is for eejits who play the lottery, but I'm sure that something means for us to be together."

Despite the reasons to do so, Alice refused to believe that it had been her who had driven Paul to swallow a bottle or two of pills and sink into a bathtub. He had demons, as Mum had noted. Demons that chased him his whole life through; demons that drove his anger and his negligence; demons that made his thoughts wander; and demons that had nothing to do with Alice. For all her myriad sins, Alice could not take this one upon herself. She had seen it so many years ago on High Street. She hadn't known what it meant: a flash of a symbol drawn in blood on a tiled wall, a wisp of Coira's raven-fire hair, the feel of the Scottish rain on her face, and the familiar pulse in her left wrist. Paths did not always make sense when they revealed themselves, but now it was as clear as day.

Alice closed her eyes as Coira napped in the stiff airplane seat. She tried to see something of her child's fate, but nothing came to her except images of Arthur. His sweet face lost so long ago in childhood. She heard his wheezing breath and felt the child's softness of his hand. She had never been skilled in seeing what lay ahead for Coira; she only dreamed it was a life free from the pain of knowing. It was a nice dream, and she said a silent prayer to whomever might listen that this time around she be granted clemency from suffering, that she be allowed the joy that threatened to be denied. Alice reached a hand out and ran it through Coira's curls. With Scotland increasingly far away, she said a soft farewell.

CHAPTER 33

CATHERINE FRASER HAD NOT *slept for three nights. On the night of the last dream, she dreamt she was walking the steep cliffs that overlooked the rocky shore some distance from here. In her dream, she was older than her present youth; she was a young woman, and her dark hair tinged with fire was long and wrapped around her as a fierce wind blew up from the sea. She was standing on a cliff overhanging a small fishing village; she could see weathered wooden boats with cloth sails made of muslin and worn rope docked at the port and bobbing up and down in the rough sea. Some distance out, a larger vessel sat, seemingly abandoned, no life apparent and a dark gloom overhanging its presence. Catherine could smell the sickly sweet rot emanating from the ship; from the town, a sense of quietly controlled panic ebbed and flowed with the rough water.*

As she stood on the cliff, she began to see a wee cabin, no more than two rooms, with a rough wooden fence surrounding it and a path laid out in rough, flat stone leading to its arched door. Smoke trickled from a chimney, and the air smelled of sage and bilberry root. In her dream,

Catherine walked down the path and opened the arched door. She was not afraid; she belonged here. Sitting at the table was a woman of unspeakable beauty with olive skin and raven hair. She looked up from her work and locked her dark eyes on Catherine; she smiled and ushered her in. Catherine felt a rush of warmth and was struck by the realization that she was dreaming—and suddenly very afraid to wake up. She crossed to the woman, who had a stack of small squares of muslin cloth in front of her. As Catherine watched, she took a drop of indigo dye from a glass bottle, and a single drop permeated the layers of cloth.

In this moment, Catherine understood that while this was a dream, it was entirely real, and as the drop of indigo dye stained layer after layer, she saw flashes of the realities that lay stacked against each other. In this moment, Catherine knew that everything was happening all at once, all at the same time, and that she was a child and an old woman simultaneously. The raven-haired woman was a whisper of smoke in the wind and flesh and blood before her. The fishing village was thriving and alive and devastated by illness and death in the same moment. She understood that there was no time, no death, and no end. She felt the vibration of the ley lines deep beneath the earth and the whisper of an ancient creature that long ago ceased to be recognizable to mortal eyes. Catherine breathed this in and opened her mouth in release, the newfound certainty releasing itself in a roar that shook the seaside cliffs and sent spikes of rocks plummeting to the water below.

Catherine woke with a start, the details of the dream already fading. Her mother ran in, startled by the little girl's screaming over what had to be a nightmare. Catherine immediately began to write down the passage of the dream, but the edges were already foggy; she forgot the color of the woman's hair and what the drop of indigo dye meant. She tried to draw the ship abandoned out at sea and strained to remember why it mattered. The only thing that stuck—what she had been doodling in her notebook for the last three days—was a strange symbol that was seemingly nothing: two jagged sets of intersecting lines creating a strange sort of unity.

The little girl drew and wrote and muttered to herself for three days while her Mum and Dad looked on. Both were medical doctors and knew that before much longer, she would need to go to the hospital. But on the third day, just as her family was preparing for the worst, Catherine closed her eyes and dropped into a dreamless sleep. Somewhere, deep in the layers of thin muslin squares, the raven-haired woman smiled to herself, and the Cailleach in her cave slumbered on.

CHAPTER 34

COIRA WAS ARRANGING HER plush animals in Alice's old bedroom. Alice had moved into Aunt Polly's recently vacated room, empty for a bit now that she had moved in with her new gentleman friend in town. Mum had rolled her eyes and held her tongue, but her silence on the subject spoke volumes.

Alice had told Coira before they left Scotland what had happened to her father, and the little girl had hardly reacted. She had shrugged and gone back to her book of dogs of the Windsors. Alice had chalked it up to shock and hadn't pressed the girl. Mum watched her with her brow furrowed.

"She does understand, doesn't she?" Mum had asked cautiously.

"I assume so," Alice answered irritably. "I don't know another way to tell her. She knows what 'dead' is. I think she's just too young to really put it all together."

Mum said that was hogwash. She poured tea and reminded Alice that she'd been no bigger when her father had died, and she had known full well what had happened.

"You sat out back of your grandmum's cottage and brought

the rain for three straight days. You didn't speak a word. The sky went black and the neighbors thought the world had gone mad," Mum said as she stared at the little girl in the next room talking softly to her stuffed bear.

"There's simply no way you can say I brought the rain, in Scotland nonetheless," Alice grumbled. She wasn't in the mood for this talk; her head was swimming with the stack of unpaid bills and paperwork from the Air Force that she had to deal with.

"I know what I know," Mum said firmly. "But that one hasn't reacted at all, for all I can see. It's not natural."

Alice stirred her tea and didn't answer. She didn't remember much of her father, just flashes of images and the smell of cinnamon. She remembered his worn work boots and riding on his shoulders as they marched down High Street. It was the clearest memory she held of him. He had balanced her on his shoulder, and they had walked to the sweet shop, where he had bought her a little cake. The cake with a little swirl of honey on top was clear as day in her mind, but her father's face, the sound of his voice, were no more substantial than a ghost. She remembered that day in the courtyard, however. She had watched the black clouds roll in from the hills, and when the rain started to fall, she had welcomed it. She remembered a feeling that her lungs were being crushed and her head would crack in two like the fairy story about the egg that fell off the wall. She knew that Coira understood what "dead" was, and she would react when she needed to and not before.

The funeral was to be held on Saturday. Paul's body had been cremated per his mother's request, and given the state of it, Alice could hardly object. It had been done before she arrived in Colorado Springs, so all Alice and Coira could say goodbye to was the grey ceramic jar that held his ashes. Mum had been incensed and grumbled that they could have at least waited a few days so his wife and daughter could say a proper goodbye. For her part, Alice was entirely numb to the decision. She had seen his face floating in the tub in the wretched basement apartment in her mind's eye. She had seen it all those years ago on the lane in Glasgow. She had no desire to see it again. As for Coira, there was no reason that Alice could see to make her last vision of her father so nightmarish. No, the grey ceramic jar was fine. Coira had reached out and run a small finger down the side. Paul's mother had sobbed, and his sister sat in a corner staring blankly. Alice and Coira had left dry-eyed, Alice feeling as though her head was detached from her body and floating on a string somewhere up above her physical form.

Alice waded through the paperwork, unraveling the mystery of who Paul had really been. She learned that he had not been transferred to a desk job as he had told her; rather, Paul had been given a medical discharge for psychiatric issues. She discovered a whole trail of incidents that went back far from the outburst on the base that she had learned about from the other wives. She learned that Paul had spent a significant amount of time covering up his life from her and from anyone else who might have cared to look. Alice read files that described fights he had gotten into on base, along with an incident where he had peed himself as he sat in the command office and then walked blankly through the compound until he had been taken to the medical unit. She learned that he had been taking painkillers, enough for the Air Force to list "persistent drug use" under the reasons for his discharge. Alice learned that nearly everything he had told her about his life on base was fabricated or glossed over in such a way that it no longer resembled the truth.

On the day of the funeral, Alice felt drained to the bone. She was angry at Paul for all the lies; she was angry she could never yell it to his face now; she was angry because he was gone and she was left with all the mess—which had been the history with him all along, Alice thought bitterly. Mum and Aunt Polly dressed Coira in a neat little dark blue dress with white trim. She twirled in the fancy clothes as though going to a party. She clutched her plush bear and stood expectantly by the door.

"You do understand where it is we're going, don't you?" Mum had asked her gently.

The little girl nodded gravely and did not speak a word.

Alice wore a smart black suit that she had made herself back at Miss Lettie's. It was another in her Jackie O series of clothes that she believed gave her invisible strength, like armor. When she had sewn it, she had envisioned wearing it to dinners and perhaps job interviews, never her husband's funeral. She methodically brushed her raven hair back and pinned it up in a thick coil at the base of her neck. She did not apply any makeup; her face was pale and nothing would hide the bags under her eyes. The four of them climbed into the car and drove to the graveyard on the edge of town. On his mother's insistence, Paul was to be interred in his family's plot, and Alice had no mind to object. She didn't care where his ashes lay. She hated them right now; they were full of lies and deceit, and they had used her and tricked her and played her for a fool.

As they stood in a small semicircle around the gravesite, the pastor read Bible passages and talked about a better place and the light of the lord. Paul's mother had wanted a church ceremony but had been denied by the priest; suicide had knocked Paul out of the kingdom of heaven as far as he was concerned. This had been one of many accusations that had been thrown at Alice leading to this day. The way Paul's mother and sister told it, if he'd never married her then he wouldn't have done this dreadful thing, and so not only had Alice killed Paul, she'd denied him everlasting life in the kingdom of heaven. Alice had rolled her eyes and kept her tongue. She didn't believe in heaven—or hell either, for that matter. One of the few things she did know with certainty about Paul was that neither did he. He may have been raised a Catholic, but he had left it behind as soon as he could.

So they had to settle for a pastor from the local Congregational church who had never met Paul and had learned of him from a written description submitted by his mother and a photograph taken by the Air Force, his uniform clean and crisp, staring straight ahead, his eyes blank. Had he been lying then? Alice thought bitterly as the pastor droned on and on about the great forgiving lord calling home his flock. Had the few letters he had sent from Vietnam been a lie too? Paul had never talked about his time there except to tell Alice one singular story.

The story went like this: Paul had been on the airstrip on the jungle base waiting for a transport helicopter to arrive. He stood watching the sky when a little girl, no more than four years old, came running out of the jungle, her face streaked with dirt and sweat. She was wearing a man's coat, far too big for her, and it dragged on the ground as her bare feet sprinted and stumbled their way to Paul. The other men on the base had seen her too and seemed to know what was happening. Paul ran toward her, his first instinct; he told Alice he had to grab her and get her away from the jungle, away from the distant sounds of gunfire. His sergeant pulled him back and tackled him to the ground, covering him with his body as the explosion rocked the sky and trees, blowing a hole in the concrete, obliterating the child, leaving only a tangle of gore and bone. It was an old tactic of the Viet

Cong, he had told Alice, and the guys who had been in-country longer than him knew the trap. They sent children with explosives strapped to them onto the bases; the men ran to help and were killed in the blast. Paul's sergeant had saved his life but lost the skin off his back and legs in the blast. The sergeant was taken to Saigon for surgery and died a week later of infection. Paul never spoke of Vietnam again, and Alice had not dared to ask.

As Alice stared at the framed portrait that sat on the gravestone, of Paul in his uniform, she wondered when it had been taken. Had he already seen the horror of a child blown to pieces in the name of war when the camera had flashed? Or had this been before he left for Vietnam? Was the blank stare part of his nature or something learned by violence and despair? Coira stood next to her, one hand tugging on the hem of Alice's dress absentmindedly and the other clutching her plush bear.

The child still hadn't cried, spoken of her father, or reacted in any way. Paul's mother had grabbed her up and held her as she cried, and Coira had simply stared at the woman as though she were an alien. "It's your doing," Paul's mother had spat at Alice days before at the funeral home as they worked out the details of the service. "Your doing." The woman's eyes narrowed and her voice sharpened. "You taught her to hate her father. Who's to say my son was even her father? Lord knows what you were up to." Alice had stifled the urge to laugh. Between the two of them, to accuse her of being the unfaithful one was ironic in a way his Welsh mother would never quite understand.

Luckily, Paul's mother and sister had been too overcome with sobs and dramatics to attack Alice since then. Two of Paul's brothers were there, quiet men who kept their heads down and spoke very little. She had never met them, and she saw no reason to be overly friendly now at this late date. The third brother was in a psychiatric hospital in Brooklyn, New York. No one had filled Alice in on the details, and she wasn't quite sure she even cared to know why. The news had prompted a mighty harrumph from Mum when she'd found out, as though this explained everything.

Alice was tired of it all. She just wanted to take her daughter and go home. Not to Mum's little cabin, but home to Glasgow. As the pastor told them to bow their heads in prayer, Alice was hit by a wave of longing for the cottage at the back of Many-Greats Grandmum Moira's manor house on Cathedral Court, where she had spent many of her early years during the war. She missed the little flat over the shop on High Street and the narrow lane framed by the laundry hung out to dry in the meager Scottish sun. She could smell the rosemary and lavender of the courtyard garden that hung on the periphery of her childhood memory. As the small crowd of mourners raised their heads from prayer and the pastor paused, Alice saw a new path for herself and Coira stretching out ahead of them.

So lost was she in her reverie that she had not noticed that the pressure of Coira's little hand had released from her skirt. She looked down and was startled to see the child was gone.

"Excuse me, young one… um, someone?" the pastor said kindly as Coira walked deliberately to the grey ceramic urn sitting on the flat board waiting to be lowered into the deep hole in the ground. Alice started to grab her back and then stopped. Her daughter needed to do whatever it was she was going to do.

The child stood in front of the urn for a long moment and then lifted her arms into the air, her teddy bear still firmly in her grip. Alice felt a stir in the air, and she exchanged a glance with Mum. Aunt Polly seemed perplexed, but despite her blood,

Aunt Polly had never been sensitive to such things. Paul's family stopped their incessant wailing and watched, unsure of what would happen next. The bleary-eyed brothers raised their heads and watched as Coira brought her arms down in a swoop, and with them an icy wind blew through the stretch of land. It carried bits of snow and sharp ice; it pushed the onlookers forward with its strength; and the grey ceramic urn tipped and cracked in half. Paul's ashes lay spread out on the board, and his mother gasped in shock. Alice stood stock-still; she had never seen any manifestation of her family's talents in Coira, and she had secretly hoped that she was as ordinary as Aunt Polly, who led a decidedly less complicated life.

The little girl flicked her wrist, and the jagged pieces of ceramic fell apart and Paul's ashes swirled into the air like a cyclone. The bits of dust and ash danced and intermingled, twinkling like stars and catching the light. Alice held her breath and the pastor fell to his knees, his eyes locked on the unimaginable sight before him. The cloud of ash grew higher and higher and then fanned out in every direction, and just like that, the mortal remains of Paul Coslet were scattered to the far ends of the wind.

"He didn't want to be in that hole," Coira said softly, turning to face her mother. "It was dark there and he hated the dark."

The next few minutes were filled with an overwhelming explosion of emotion and angry words. Alice rushed to her daughter, followed by Mum and Aunt Polly, who folded the little girl into their protective arms and blocked her from the rage of Paul's mother, who unleashed a torrent of curses that made the pastor cringe. The sister's passive state had broken as well, and she threw herself at Alice. She screamed that this was all her doing, that Alice was behind this and it was evil, Satan's work, and they would rot in hell. The pastor sat on the ground, stunned and speechless.

Later, after Coira had been fed a plate of liver and onions by Mum, bathed, and tucked into her clean bed that used to be Alice's, they all sat around the great dark wood table and Mum poured a length of brandy into each of their tea cups. No one had much to say; even Aunt Polly was speechless. Alice sipped the dark liquor and unconsciously ran her fingers over the ink mark on her left wrist. Mum was doing the same, staring into her cup.

"I spent a good part of my life trying to figure how to shield you from this," Mum said finally. "I thought by bringing you here, away from the old country, that you would grow to be different, ordinary." She glanced at Aunt Polly. "No offense intended."

"None taken," Aunt Polly said with a slight smirk on her lips. "The lot of you are creepy enough without me adding to the mix." Despite herself, Alice smiled at her aunt's plump face, which was starting to show an elaborate cross pattern of wrinkles.

"I thought that if I never taught you about the old ways, the things your Great-Grandmum Muriel taught me, then you would be safe from it all." She paused. "I've known since you were Coira's size that I'd failed, and then I failed doubly by not stepping in later on."

"Mum—" Alice began, but Mum cut her off.

"No. Let me finish. There's a thing we're meant to remember in our line, something that has always felt just out of reach for me and something that seems to be getting stronger with each one of us. My Grandmum knew it, and it was just outside her grasp. That little one in there is stronger than all of us put together."

And just like that, Alice found herself and Coira back on a plane for another seven-hour journey, to be followed by another eight-hour journey. This time there were no tears. Mum sat next to them, helping Coira arrange her colors on the airplane tray. Aunt Polly had taken over the cabin in the woods; she might sell it, she told them, buy a condo somewhere it doesn't snow. She had kissed them all goodbye, and Mum had left knowing her baby sister did not need her protection any longer.

In the blackness of her cave, the Cailleach raised her head to listen to the still air and rustle of insect legs on the stone walls. The dark waters of the Lethe splashed along the banks, and she knew her daughters were finally arriving home.

CHAPTER 35

CATHERINE FRASER HAS BEEN suspended from the primary school for one week. The incident started as a fuss over nothing, in her opinion, but Mum and Dad have not seen it that way. She had fallen asleep during arithmetic—not on purpose—but the instructor, an old man who spoke with a lisp and smelled of tuna fish, had been droning on and on about long division, and she had nodded clean off.

That was not what led to her suspension, however. The suspension came somewhat later as the old man was making Catherine clean the chalkboards and sweep the floor of the classroom as punishment for sleeping through the lesson. The other students had left for the day, and Catherine knew her Mum was expecting her at the college any time now. She normally walked from the primary school to Queen Margaret's Medical College for Women, where her mother was a lecturer. The old man knew this and highly disapproved, as did many old men who encountered her mother; they believed that she had greatly overstepped her boundaries by becoming a teacher in what was traditionally a man's field. Catherine suspected that her punishment had less to do with her sleeping and more to do with a grudge held against her on her mother's behalf.

Even now, as she pounded erasers in the open window sending clouds of yellow chalk dust flying, he was sitting at his great wooden desk that was said to be modeled after Prime Minister Baldwin's writing table and muttering half to himself and half to Catherine about what exactly her problem was. It was, according to his sputtering rant, a lack of direction at home, two working parents, and no one at home to teach her the proper ways of discipline and manners. And don't get him started on her grandmother, and don't think we don't all know about where you come from, young lady. Catherine set down the newly dusted erasers and picked up two more, creating a yellow chalk cloud to block out his words.

We all know what goes on in that shop, he was ranting. Selling snake oil and spitting in the eye of the Church is what goes on there. He slammed down a geometry book in the guise of straightening up his papers. Catherine had heard all this before and was still largely tuning him out. Her Grandmum Muriel ran the apothecary that had been owned by her great-grandmother, everyone in town knew that. Everyone also knew that Many-Greats Grandmum Moira's grand house had become a girl's boarding school when she passed away at the grand age of ninety-eight. The boarding school was extremely selective and taught the girls unheard-of things such as science and the medicinal arts. Catherine and her mother were often the target of much ire from the more traditional crowd who believed their family was destroying the very structure of things. Mum laughed at such talk; she was quite used to it. She had spent her entire career being an exception to the rule, and the crass comments rolled off her like water off a duck's back.

Catherine was not quite as accustomed to it all, though. The old man stood and crossed to a stack of student papers on the sideboard. If the authorities had done their job, he continued, they'd have run your line out of town in accordance with the witching laws. You do know about the witching laws, don't you, girl? he asked with a sneer on his thin lips surrounded by shoots of grey mustache hair. Tell me, Miss Fraser, what exactly are the witchcraft laws? He was assuming she didn't know. Catherine sighed. She knew the laws well; the old man was not the first instructor to bring them up in a lecture in the name of history and then spend the lesson shooting challenging looks at her. She had been told about the Witchcraft Act of 1735 by her Grandmum Muriel and Great-Grandmum Catriona. She knew that the shop where they worked and lived was officially an apothecary that sold teas and herbs for the bath and whatnot. She knew that the officials largely looked the other way, and when they did not, bribes had been known to be paid. She also knew that there was much talk about dropping the Witchcraft Act from the books, and that no one had enforced the law for so many years that most didn't even know it existed. The old man, however, assumed strongly that she did not know any of this and that the mere mention of witchcraft laws would make her quake in her Mary Janes. The assumption angered her.

And your sister, the old man continued. Don't think that we don't know exactly the cause of that calamity. At this, Catherine began to feel the water stop rolling off her back and begin to saturate her skin. The devil's work if ever I've seen it, he continued.

Catherine stopped wiping the chalkboard with a damp cloth and stood facing the green scratched surface, trying to breathe as Mum had taught her to do when she became angry. Polly had been born in a caul, an suspicious sign if ever there was one among the older and less educated circle in town. Mum had been at the NHS hospital where Dad worked in the children-and-family ward. Catherine and Dad had sat in the waiting room while the nurses and doctors ran back and forth, so the story that came to them concerning Polly had been secondhand.

The nurses cut the caul from the baby's head to find her blue and devoid of breath. A slap to her arse did nothing, and it was all the nurses could do to wrap the poor wee thing in a blanket and hand the dead infant to Mum. The rest of the story came from a young Red Cross volunteer who paused to look back, as the rest excused themselves from the tragedy. The girl, who would later tell the story to the whole of Glasgow from what it seemed, was shaken: it was the first stillborn infant she had seen, and she was trying not to cry, as it might upset the mother. But the mother of the dead infant wasn't crying; instead, she sang a song in a language that the Red Cross girl didn't recognize. It was less song and more chant, and as her voice droned on and on, the young onlooker found herself locked into place as though by witchcraft.

What happened next was most certainly the strongest evidence of ill deeds and dark spirits (as goes the story that spread across town). The tiny blue-grey corpse lying in her mother's arms began to move, and then the skin began to change. No more was it the color of death itself, but a healthy pink. The tiny face, frozen in death, came to life, and a mighty scream broke from the infant's lips. The mother, who should have been terrified and fearful, instead lay there as calm as though she were knitting a sweater. She held the baby and whispered something the Red Cross girl could not quite make out, but it most certainly was not English and without doubt was the devil's work.

The doctors rushed back in to hear the crying baby and declared a miracle. Later, after Polly was safe at home in their cottage set back in the woods a distance from the manor house on Cathedral Court, lookie-loos peeked through the front window, already full of the story the young Red Cross girl had told a dozen people. Those dozen had each told a dozen more, and soon it seemed the whole of Glasgow knew the strange story of how Mum had brought baby Polly back to life. Mum chuckled and ignored the curious eyes and questions. Dad bristled and ignored the attention, but Catherine felt a surge of protectiveness toward her little sister, born in a caul and never meant to hold breath. She would not let her be marred by such ugly whispers and thoughts.

The old man continued on. Witchery if I've ever seen it, and no better than the ones that came before you. Wouldn't be surprised if the lot of you end up on the pyre. Catherine felt a slow boil starting in her toes. It rolled up her calves and knees, up into her belly, where it settled and shot like a dart to her temples. Back in the day, they took witches to the edge of town and collected a pile of stones and you can guess what happened next. The old man spat out the words as he slammed textbooks down on his writing table. They'd start with your witch of a grandmother and torch her snake-oil shop. Catherine spun around, locking her dark eyes on the old man's watery blue. He paused, but seeing her anger, he lifted his thin upper lip in a sneer of victory. Next they'd haul your witch of a mother out into the street, tie her to a stake, and light a match. Catherine felt her fists balling up; the old man was waiting for her to scream, to cry, to insult him. If she did, it wouldn't be pounding erasers and sweeping the floor, it would be far more serious, and a voice in Catherine's head warned her about taking the bait.

Next they'd march to that witch house and throw all those young ghouls out by the napes of their necks. Nothing but trouble, educating girls, and they'll all grow up to be exactly like the rotten lot that you call family. Catherine closed her eyes, counting to ten as her mother had taught her. The voice droned on and on from behind the writing table. You and your sister would be sent to the workhouses; see if that weak little sack of a girl can lift and pull, or if God would take back what was never meant to be here in the first place.

Catherine's eyes snapped open, and she felt the pulse in her temples flowing down her arms. Her eyes fixed on the old man, and instead of a sneer, she saw fear in his aged eyes. The papers and books flew from his desk as though they had a mind of their own. The writing table overturned, spilling a teacup and a metal ruler that he used to smack the hands of lazy students. The old man let out a sound that would've been a scream if he had had enough breath. It was Catherine's turn to smile.

"I'm done cleaning, sir," she said quietly in a voice she did not quite recognize and walked out the door.

Mum had listened to the headmaster's story of how Catherine had thrown papers and books around the room and flipped a desk with her bare hands. Catherine had managed to suppress a laugh at the old man's version of the story and at the fear in his eyes as he avoided her stare. Catherine would not go back to the public primary school; instead, she was enrolled in her many-greats grandmum's academy even though she was the youngest student in the crowd. It was, strictly speaking, a secondary school, but the headmistress didn't bat an eye. I'm sure that a girl of your talents will make your family proud, was all she said.

Catherine Fraser didn't learn witchery in the classrooms set in what used to be Moira Blair's sitting room and bedrooms. She learned chemistry and biology, she grew plants in the greenhouse set in the back garden, and she learned Latin and French. She passed her old primary school every so often when she was sent out on errands and could not resist slamming the old man's windows shut with a flick of her wrist when she saw him standing by the old writing desk. He always jumped, and Catherine always laughed to see it. The vibration in her mind and hands was ancient and powerful. Deep somewhere in the lowland crags, an ancient hag stirred slightly and slumbered on. All was quiet for now, but she knew a great awakening was nigh. The Cailleach settled in for a final rest before the dawn; the promise of Ingwaz that had stood for thousands of years was coming round. The ancient line of hags was beginning to remember, and soon they would cross Lethe and into the light.

CHAPTER 36

ON THE LONGEST NIGHT *of the year, when the wind howled through the streets of Glasgow, Catherine dreamt she was sitting by a fire in a great stone hearth. She was wrapped in layers of rough cloth, and still she shivered. Her house was empty and it smelled of death. She knew that inside the bedroom behind her lay the body of a man she loved dearly, his death shroud neatly sewn around him; he lay quiet and still, the deformities brought on by illness and pain hidden by the smooth muslin cloth. She knew that she was the only living person in the entire village; the rest were as dead as the man in the next room was. In her dream, she stared into the fire and knew that a ship full of rotting corpses sat a short distance from the docks, the sickness that had destroyed the village festering and growing within its rotting shell.*

As she sat by the fire, the sound of the waves crashing outside her door and a storm born of grief and loss whipping through the hills, she stared into the fire and saw a young woman walking with a group of robed priestesses. In her dream state, Catherine felt a rush of gratitude that this young woman had escaped the sight of such atrocity. She also felt the great raw patch on her heart that the girl's departure had left. As the fire snapped and popped in the hearth, Catherine sat still and watched as an entire life was played out without the burden of lost memories. She saw the cabin on the cliffs and the fire-haired, coral-eyed girl walking down to the village. She saw everything: a man who had no idea his lost daughter had come home to him, a happy sort of existence for a time. She felt a rush of heat through her body as she brushed hands with a young man who would become her husband. She felt the firmness of her belly and the sharp stab of a tiny foot beating its way into her ribs.

As Catherine slept, she understood that this was no ordinary dream but a window into yet another layer of the cloth. She understood that this reality was happening alongside hers, and in the same breath was long past and nothing but a memory. The two worlds spun alongside each other, neither more nor less real than the other. In her dreams, she understood the woman's pain as though it were her own. As the fire licked and devoured the wood and kindling, Catherine knew that this woman and the one on the cliffs and those who had come before her were all squares of thin muslin cloth stacked on top of each other, each reality a drop of ink left to permeate and stain the layers below. Catherine closed her eyes and let the realization of this truth overwhelm her. On her forearm she felt a gentle burning sensation and looked down to see the two sets of jagged lines intersecting with each other inked onto her left wrist. She was descended from something greater than man, and as the fire warmed the tiny cottage and the sea raged outside, Catherine understood the weight of her blood.

Morning came, and she immediately grabbed the small notebook next to her bed and wrote down as many details as she remembered, but the sensations and the clarity were already fading. She drew the symbol that had appeared and tried to describe the smell of death, the sound of the waves, the unknowable reality that she was alone, all the others she had ever known dead and rotting. Mum frowned when she recounted the dream over breakfast and dug out an old family Bible with names listed in the margins. The jagged, intersecting lines appeared over and over, and Catherine stared at them in fascination.

Later that day on her way to the baker, she waved her hand and slammed the windows of the old man's classroom just to see him jump. He shot a glare in her direction, and Catherine smiled and waved as was her customary response. It was becoming easier and easier to channel her intent into a flick of her wrist or twirl of her hand. Grandmum Muriel had noticed and responded with an uneasy agreement that she was to come to the shop after school from now on for extra tutoring. More than lessons, they examined the old Bible and listed the names that lay inside. Each generation of women had added the names of their mother and children, and the list seemed endless. Catherine and Grandmum listed each and tried to put it all into order, tracing the symbol with the jagged lines as they talked and discussed.

She was starting to remember, and soon she would find herself on the far banks of the Lethe laden with the knowledge of her lineage. But for now they drank strong black tea and sounded out the ancient names of a line of hags whose reach far surpassed their understanding. The winter winds screamed past the door to the little shop on High Street, and deep in her cave, the Cailleach slumbered on.

CHAPTER 37

THE ONCE-GRAND HOUSE on Cathedral Court was in ruins. Mum gasped and held on to Alice to steady herself. After Grandmum Rowan's passing, Mum had hired a caretaker for the ancient manor, but it was clear he had been negligent in his duties and spent more time at the Saltmarket pubs than he had tending the house. The last time they had seen it was when Coira had been just an infant, and Mum and Aunt Polly had flown across the ocean to visit her. It had been a boarding house then, and apart from a somewhat-neglected yard, it had seemed to be in good shape. That, however, had been years ago, and now the stone exterior was stained and crumbling in places. The fine shrubberies and foliage out front were brown and dry. The real horror was the inside. The caretaker had stopped vetting his tenants long ago; he lived in the cottage on the far end of the property and paid no mind to the parties and drugs that had come and gone in the big house. Many-Greats Grandmum Moira's front parlor walls were speckled with holes and covered with graffiti. A mattress stained with unimaginable fluids was on the floor. The kitchen, which Alice remembered from her childhood with Grandmum Rowan, was a wreck. The sink was lined with a black mold that would be impossible to clean. The stove was missing entirely, and the cooler stood open, obviously not used for some time.

The caretaker clearly had not expected anyone to ever come back and did not even wait for Mum's line of curses and demands for explanations. He had left before they arrived, leaving the cottage empty and usable for the time being. The old man had miraculously been collecting rent, albeit a pittance, up until the time the last official boarder had left, which had been shortly before Mum had written him to let him know they were returning.

It was shocking that so much damage could be done in so short a time; not that many years had passed since the closure of the girl's school and Grandmum Rowan's passing, but, as Mum reminded Alice, Grandmum Rowan had never lived in the big house. She and Granddad had always preferred the cottage on the edge of the property. The decline had most likely started as soon as the school closed and the boarders arrived; the parties and neglect had escalated the process. The neighbors were grateful that there was an end to the madness that had ensued; they'd issued complaints with the polis so often that they had stopped coming out to write them up. It's about time, they said to Mum and Alice; it's about time it was a proper house.

As had been true in its heyday, the grand manor house on Cathedral Court was the subject of vast and varied rumors and stories. Even in the last few years, when dirty syringes and filth had collected in the corners, local children had dared each other to sneak up the cracked and broken stone walkway and peek in the window. Alice worried about Coira, who was so little, newly five years old. Would she be scared of the old place? All the worry was for naught, however. She stood on the stone steps, looking up at the grey stone spires and arched doorway, and smiled. She had always been a quiet child and had hardly spoken since her father had died. Alice worried about her greatly, but she knew that some things are only healed with time and space.

Mum had a sizable check from her half of the sale of the cabin in Colorado Springs. As Alice and Coira cleaned and settled the back cottage, Mum hired a crew to gut the house and begin the extensive job of renovating the sad exterior. The three of them settled into the little cottage that Alice remembered from her childhood. In her memory, she could still hear the dull rumble of far-off explosions. The table, which she had huddled under with Grandmum Rowan, was still there in the tiny dining room. There were only two bedrooms, so Alice held Coira tight to her as they slept in the narrow bed.

Alice had fallen asleep as soon as her head hit the pillow. Between the move and the house and getting Coira settled, she could barely keep her eyes open when it fell dark. Alice sat up in bed. Coira was still curled into a tiny ball, her chest rising and falling in perfect rhythm. She could hear Mum's soft snores in the bedroom next door. The ink mark on her wrist pulsed and throbbed, and she rubbed it absently as she looked around the room. The moon was unnaturally bright; the entire room was lit as though the sun had risen. Alice shook her head. She did not remember that being the case when they had gone to bed. Careful not to wake her daughter, Alice crawled over the little girl and pulled a soft knit blanket around her own shoulders. Her feet bare, she padded out into the main room. The cottage was still and quiet, but there was something not quite settled. She walked to the door and turned the knob. The elm and birch trees that lined the land reflected the unnatural brightness of the moon. As though entranced, Alice stepped out onto the rough dirt and began walking to the main house.

The manor house rose up before her as she remembered it from her childhood. The perfectly sculpted stone spires and grand archways, the meticulous molding on the awning, and the prim and manicured shrubs and flowers lay before her. Alice shook her head. The house began to glow, and Alice realized that the light she had attributed to the moon was emanating from the house itself. The very stone was giving off starlight, and the sight made Alice draw in her breath and wrap the blanket tightly around her shoulders. It was terrifying, but also beautiful and familiar. She could hear a low hum coming from the stones and glass. She took a step forward, pulled from her gut toward the structure that seemed to heave and vibrate with its own breath.

Alice opened her eyes with a start. Her body was rigid and her fists clenched. The moon was no more bright or dull than it should be. Coira slept next to her, undisturbed. Alice sat up and looked out the window at the thick grove of elms and willows. A dream; that was all it had been. A dream that had seemed absurdly real. It was the stress, she repeated to herself. Next to her, Coira stirred and looked up at her.

"I'm sorry, love, I didn't mean to wake you," Alice whispered, brushing a strand of raven-black hair with a bite of fire from her forehead.

"It's not time yet, Momma," Coira said simply. It was more than she had spoken since they arrived, and Alice was startled to hear her small, sweet voice.

"Not time for what, darling?" Alice asked quietly, lying back down and propping her head on her elbow so she could look directly into Coira's honey-brown eyes.

"She hasn't woken up yet. But soon. She talks to me in my dreams. Don't be afraid," Coira said, and without offering any further explanation, she turned and curled back up into a ball, her plush teddy bear pressed to her chest.

Alice stared at the ceiling and tried to make sense of it all. The tiny mark of the intersecting jagged lines pulsed. She suspected that the little girl was more powerful than all the women in her family put together. She listened and watched with an intensity that unsettled others and that Alice recognized as a step in gathering her strength.

Coira spent her days in the wooded patch that surrounded the cottage, sending dandelion fluff sailing through the air so thickly it looked like snow while she twirled and danced, a contented smile on her face. One day, a spin of crisp leaves flew over her head in a cyclone much like the release of Paul's ashes back in Colorado. It spun higher and higher, creating a wind that made the workmen over at the main house look to the sky and climb down from their ladders. Alice knew that a simple truth was looming. Someone had to teach her how to use this. She did not know where to begin. All the things she had ever been capable of had happened without her knowledge of how or why they existed. The children back in the classroom in Los Angeles; the men on the street in Caracas. All these things happened out of a sense of anger and survival.

Coira, however, seemed to have no anger in her. Her eyes had aged a century since her father died, and the honey-brown innocence had been replaced with something else, but it was not anger. No, Coira looked as though she were waiting, biding her time. Whoever spoke to her in her dreams was not awake yet, and Alice tried not to shiver when she repeated the little girl's words in her mind.

Alice lay in bed and eventually fell back into a deep and dreamless sleep. It was not time yet, and of all the uncertainty they lived with, she knew beyond a doubt that the day that her daughter truly awakened would leave little time for rest.

CHAPTER 38

ONE MORNING, NOT TOO long before they were able to move into the big house, Alice woke to find Coira and Mum sitting at the table with a small stack of squares of cloth in front of them. Next to that was a small inkbottle. The combination of the two seemingly disconnected things made Alice stop in her tracks and stare, the words caught in her throat.

"It's not entirely right," Mum explained apologetically. "I can't show her the same way I was shown. I saw this in a dream, you see, a dream from a long time ago, a dream I believe was sent to me by one of our line."

Alice sat down across from the pair and watched as Mum showed Coira the stack of cloth, the pieces all lined up with each other, layer upon layer. Using a dropper, she leaked a single drip of black ink onto the topmost layer. "See how it moves," Mum said to Coira, who sat stock-still, watching. "All time is stacked up on top of each other; the things that happen to us, the births and deaths and everything in between, is happening at the same time." Mum spoke slowly, trying to make sense out of it herself as she explained it to the silent child. "My many-greats grandmum is up there in her house right now, and it's the grandest manor in all of Glasgow. We are living there right now, too. You have a bedroom the size of this entire cottage." Mum smiled at her granddaughter. "Your animals are all lined up on your bed; you're taking a nap maybe. That's right here on this layer of cloth, and all the other people who have lived in the house, the revelers who left all their trash behind, are still there. Your Great-Grandmum Rowan is off at war; your mum is a little girl in Colorado Springs. It's all happening on top of each other. Everything we do is like this drop of ink: it leaks to the next layer of time and reality and leaves a mark, and sometimes we don't know quite what it means."

Alice sat mesmerized, watching Mum explain the unexplainable to her granddaughter. Coira took it all in with her great, ancient honey eyes. Her plush bear sat in the chair next to her. In some ways, she was older than all of them; in others, she was still a child.

"It's too much, Mum," Alice said softly.

"We don't have time," Mum said quietly, locking her eyes on Alice. "I already failed a score by not teaching you what I knew. I thought I could protect you, that if you didn't know, you'd live an ordinary life like your aunt. My mum's gifts were different; her sight was subtler and she showed me what she could, but it wasn't near enough. I learned from your Great-Grandmum Muriel, and I learned about things she had done that made me want to close it all down. I tried to shut it all out, ignore it, cast it aside, but I see now that the danger comes in closing our eyes to it, not bringing it into the open."

Coira listened to all this intently. Alice sat speechless and still. Coira took the ink dropper and let a black point of ink fall to the stack of cloth.

"It's almost time," she said, then stood, taking her bear outside to dance with the butterflies.

CHAPTER 39

THE NEEDLE STINGS AND *bites, but Catherine sits as still as she can.*

"C'mon now, love, this is just a tiny little mark. Think about the state you'd be in if you were really letting me work!" The woman with the bob cut and lines of ink running up and down her arms and chest giggled softly. Catherine's left wrist was outstretched, and the woman was meticulously inking the symbol of the intersecting jagged lines into the soft flesh. She ran her shop not far from Grandmum Muriel's on High Street. Grandmum frequently sold her crèmes and lotions to soothe the freshly inked skin and relieve pain. When Catherine told Grandmum what she felt she must do, Muriel had sighed and then led her to the woman with the bob cut and bright eyes, who had carefully examined the symbol that Catherine had etched out on a notepad.

"Runes," she had said simply.

Catherine had nodded. She had been researching the runes and their meaning in the Girls' Academy library as well as at Queen Margaret College while she waited for Mum to be done teaching for the day.

Catherine had not been able to explain the urge she had except that it appeared over and over in the dreams that felt more real than her daily life. Mum was strictly against it; the idea of a woman getting tattooed like a circus freak was beyond her understanding. Grandmum Muriel had been a bit more understanding about it and had listened quietly while Catherine recounted the dreams that had barraged her sleep for the last few months.

There are stories, secrets, that your great-grandmum and I kept that your mother does not know. If you're meant to know them, then the dreams will lead you to it; but if not, perhaps it's better if they are forgotten, Grandmum Muriel had said quietly. Catherine had known better than to press her for details.

Catherine's dream journal was nearly full; the images had been coming nightly, and she woke feeling as though she had hardly slept. Mum worried about her and said she was too worked up about this, that she gave it far too much credence and it was going to drive her mad. Examinations were coming up, Mum said with a deep furrow between her eyes. It was Mum's hope that Catherine would follow in her footsteps, test into the college, study medicine or science. For her part, Catherine liked the quiet life that Grandmum Muriel led. She liked the lotions and oils made from the herb garden in the courtyard. She liked the narrow lane and the tiny shop and never felt so at-home as she did in the little flat overhead. She could sit in the window and watch people walk to and fro, a scene barely changed in a hundred years' time; it was as though you were in a time warp. "Fit to be torn down" was how Mum described it, but Catherine quietly disagreed. For her, there was no greater place, and she did not need examination scores to run that little shop and live in the spare bedroom with Grandmum Muriel.

"Almost done," the woman with the bob cut and deft hands said. "If you don't mind me asking, what's the significance of this to ya? Most

of my clients are wanting something a bit showier, if ya know what I mean."

Catherine winced as the needle bit and stung and told the woman about the Norse god Ing and the promise of peace and completion.

"It's about cycles, and as mad as it sounds, I feel like I'm part of a grand cycle, all the women who came before me, and when I have a daughter of my own, it will all come round to where it began." Catherine paused. The woman simply nodded in understanding and stayed at her work. She had explained this to Polly the night before when Polly had tried to talk her out of it. Polly was still in the primary school and sure she was to be terribly embarrassed by her sister's actions.

"All right," the woman with the bob cut said with finality. She gave Catherine a lotion in a glass bottle that came from Grandmum Muriel's shop: comfrey and lavender to combat the inflammation and fight irritation. Catherine smiled; she had made this batch herself, grinding the herbs with a mortar and pestle at the long worktable in the back of the shop.

She looked at her wrist. The flesh surrounding the mark was red and angry, but Catherine felt an energy run through her veins that she had never felt before. It was a sort of pulse that began in her blood and raced out to her fingers, her toes, and the top of her head. She was not the first to bear this mark, she knew; somewhere the tradition had been lost, and now remembered was not to be forgotten.

CHAPTER 40

POLLY IS LEAVING FOR *the United States. She was barely settled into the Girls' Academy when she made the declaration. "In love," she said, to a boy with a ridiculous mustache and a cousin in Colorado, United States. Mum raged about the kitchen and even broke several dinner plates while Dad sat quietly as his face turned varying shades of red and purple. Catherine had moved out of the cottage the year before, secondary school complete; her examination scores had qualified her for university, but to Mum's dismay, she had declined the opportunity. Grandmum Muriel needed help; she could no longer manage the steps down to the shop on her own, and the daily work and running of the business was getting to be too much. Catherine went to live with her and take over the shelves of lotions and oils. Grandmum Muriel taught her everything about the herbs and roots. She learned how to keep the tiny rows of green leaves healthy and strong, and the courtyard had never looked so vibrant. Mum had resigned herself to her daughter's choice with surprisingly little fight, as though she had been expecting it all along.*

Polly's decision, however, was beyond comprehension. Are you pregnant? Dad raged from his chair, his voice ragged and raw. Is that why you have to take off all of a sudden and leave? Polly had stood her ground. She wasn't pregnant; she was in love and was going to marry the boy with the ridiculous mustache who had been offered a job fixing airplanes at a great air academy in a town on the other side of the world. You can't stop me, she said defiantly. She was right, and that was that. Catherine had tried to talk to her after the initial row, but there was no sense to be had of it. You'll thank me one day, she said. You'll thank me that I'm going; we'll all be there together and leave this place. She waved her hand at the grey Scottish sky.

Polly and the boy with the ridiculous mustache were married that June and sailed for the United States the following week. Mum and Grandmum Muriel made a cake with chocolate frosting, and the neighbors came to share a glass of brandy and congratulate the new couple, toasting them in the sprawling garden of the Girls' Academy. It was a small affair, and Catherine felt her heart breaking the entire time. The baby who had been born in a caul, far on the other side of death and brought back to life by her mother's ancient words, was leaving them all. Polly had never had any interest in the herbs or plants, nor did she have the dreams that still followed Catherine or the ability to move objects with the simple swish of her hand or a concentrated stare. She was outrageously ordinary, and in many ways Catherine envied her mundanity. She was moving on to live an ordinary life with a man who would take an ordinary job. They would live next to other ordinary people who would never whisper about her family or cross themselves when they walked past. Glasgow is a superstitious town, Mum had always told her. Industry and hard work had left people to suspect anything that was different; so it had been so many years ago when Many-Greats Grandmum Moira first lived in her grand house, and so it was now.

Catherine had learned to better hide her abilities. Grandmum Muriel taught her to breathe deep and focus her energy. She taught her to read the runes and songs that would soothe the fussiest baby or calm the angriest adult. She taught her the magic of herbs and plants and everything she had been taught by her mum, Great-Grandmum Catriona, for whom Catherine had been named. She taught her granddaughter how to listen to the voices of the dead and how to summon spirits. And she asked her every morning, while Catherine made her a cup of thick, black tea, about her dreams: Had she dreamt of the rowan tree outside of town? Grandmum Muriel would ask. Catherine had not and knew that the ancient tree for which Mum was named held a secret that, if meant for her to know, would reveal itself in time.

Polly wrote letters full of ordinary news. They had moved into a little house in Colorado Springs, Colorado. They had a yard and a ginger cat named Penelope. She volunteered at the church, and her new husband worked alongside his cousin at an air yard learning how to repair planes to be used in the American Air Force. Polly made dishes for potluck suppers and hosted teas for the other ladies in the neighborhood. She wrote to Catherine that she was trying to rid herself of her Scottish accent and be more American. Catherine sat in her room in the flat over the shop on High Street and felt her heart drop a bit. Polly was forgetting everything about where she had come from.

The shop was entirely Catherine's now. Grandmum Muriel preferred to sit in her rocking chair at the window and watch the people go to and fro in the lane. Catherine worried about her at times but knew that she was neither ill nor unhappy. She was content to rest now that it was clear her work was to be carried on. She had done the same for her mother, Great-Grandmum Catriona, until she had passed peacefully in the night and the shop had become hers. Now, Catherine would take over when Grandmum Muriel crossed to the next world. Her work complete,

Catherine knew she was waiting for the drop of ink to saturate the cloth. When it touched the square on which she existed, she would close her eyes and move to the next world.

CHAPTER 41

THE FIRST NIGHT IN the great house, Alice could feel the energy swirling. The paint was fresh, the walls newly patched, and the floor polished to a high shine. The chandelier in the dining room had been replaced, and the furniture was tasteful and simple, much of it donations from the Historical Society that was delighted that the old manor was being revived. Coira had immediately walked every inch of the house and chosen her room. Mum had gotten a curious expression on her face, and later she told Alice that the little room in the back overlooking the grounds had been, according to what she knew of the house's history, the secondary parlor where Moira Blair used to hold her séances back in the day. It wasn't the largest room by far, and Alice had asked Coira if she was sure. The little girl had nodded, satisfied.

On that first night, Alice could not sleep. She rose from her bed, missing the warm weight of her daughter sleeping next to her. She rose and walked downstairs and stood in the newly revived kitchen. New stove, new cooler, new sink and counter; it looked like a magazine spread. She poured herself a glass of milk and sat at the little wooden table, moved over from the cottage. Alice wondered how long this could last, this fairy-tale life. Paul's pension from the Air Force helped, and they had the funds that had been collected from the boarding house, but Alice knew she could not pretend that it would last forever. Money, as it had frequently done, worked its way into a pit of worry in her stomach. Coira would need to start primary school soon; how would she manage? She was an odd child, growing odder by the day. And Mum. The women in her family enjoyed great old age, but Mum was sleeping more and more, moving less, and starting to get lost staring into space. How long would she be with them? And how would Alice handle the loss? Paul's death had been a combination of shock and inevitability; Mum's would tear her heart out.

Placing the cup carefully back in the stainless steel sink, Alice turned off the light and walked from room to room. It was unreal that this was her house now, the place she lived. Her childhood in Glasgow was muddy, the years in the flat over the shop and then later, during the war, in the cottage with Grandmum. She thought of her father; she'd had a dream of him the other night, nothing supernatural, just a string of disconnected memories, her brain sorting out information and trying to put it in the right order. She saw a flash of hazel green eyes and the pair of old work boots he kept by the door. He had been lost in the war, as had most of the fathers and husbands back in those dark days. As Alice stood in the doorway to the study, now furnished with a replica King George IV writing table courtesy of the Historical

Society, she wondered what he would have thought about all this.

She didn't quite understand why Mum had ever left Scotland. She'd never belonged in America, not really. And Aunt Polly was never quite as fragile as Mum assumed her to be. Tiny, yes, but not fragile, not like Arthur had been. She supposed it had been the war that really drove her to leave. Cathedral Court had been spared the worst of it, and Alice's memories of the rubble, the smoke, and the ashes were hazy. Aunt Polly had promised that children were playing in the streets, that the world was safe in America. And in some ways she had been right.

However, as the energy of the house zigged and zagged its way around the newly rebuilt walls in a house that prompted everyone who passed to whisper about spirits and ghouls, Alice knew that no place was ever really safe. Children died in the night, choking on their own lungs; men swallowed bottles of pills and drowned in a tub; and mothers closed their eyes and never woke up. Alice's paths were hidden from her now; all she could see were the dark wood floors and arched doorways of her many-greats grandmother's manor. Upstairs, her daughter slept and spoke in riddles, and somewhere a great distance away, in the lowland crags, the Cailleach opened her eyes to stare into the darkness.

CHAPTER 42

CATHERINE DREAMT OF THE *rowan tree on the shortest night of the year as winds whipped up and down High Street and snow covered the cobblestones. The unlucky souls who had left their wash out on the line crossing the narrow lane had lost it to the torrential gusts of winter wind and snow. In her dream it was spring, and the flowers had just begun to poke up from the winter soil. Somewhere a wedding was taking place, and Catherine was glad that it was a clear day. As she looked out over the field, the rowan tree on the edge of the woods glowed with an ethereal light as though it was lit up from within. A ferocious strike of lightning crackled down from the sky, hovering over the woods and locking on its target. Catherine fell back and felt a searing pain run from her heart to the bottom of her feet. The ground around her crackled with electricity, blue currents of light running through the rough grass and winding their way around the dog's mercury and dandelions. She heard a scream that was far older than the rowan tree or the woods surrounding them. It was a cry that stretched from a great distance and was more ancient than the city ports or the walls of the burg. It was anger and fear and grief of the deepest sort that cannot be expressed through anything other than rage.*

Catherine sat up to see black storm clouds rolling in and covering every inch of light from the sun. It was midnight in an instant. The rowan tree shed its leaves and turned to ash where it stood. The ground shook and trembled. An inhuman cry of rage filled the air, matching the cracks of lightning and the responding rolls of thunder. Catherine shook to see a wave of sorts rising from where the rowan tree had stood. The ground surged and rolled as though a great force was just underneath the topmost layer of soil. In its wake, the field grass and spring flowers withered and turned to ash to match the rowan tree. Catherine rose to her feet as the surge of earth and ash reached where she stood. It moved around her, the scorched soil dying beneath her toes. It traveled rapidly across the field to the city port, and a sickening realization washed over Catherine as she realized what the ash and soil were bringing to the city. She felt her lungs burning with the sickness and saw great clods of blood coughed up from her chest. She felt a fever burning and the terror as all those touched by the illness stared at the midnight sky, waiting for death.

She woke with a start. The night was clear and her chest was healthy and strong. As she lay in her room next to the window, she looked out at the stars and knew what it was that Grandmum Muriel had kept from her and Mum all this time. She understood the power that had been unleashed on that terrible spring day. A crash from the next room jolted her from her bed. Grandmum Muriel was sitting up, staring at the far wall.

"I didn't know how to control it," Muriel murmured.

Catherine moved to her and sat on the edge of the narrow bed.

"She sent it from the lowlands, and I carried it to town. I hated them all. I wanted every last one of them to die, and they did." Grandmum Muriel's voice was rhythmic, an intonation. "I don't remember, child."

She turned and grabbed Catherine's hands in her own, pushing up her nightgown sleeve to reveal the small tattoo on her left wrist. "I don't remember what it means, but you must, and you must teach your daughter."

Catherine was shaking. So much death, so much pain. She could still feel the burning in her throat as the blood rose from her lungs, choking and drowning her. She felt the weight of the limp bodies of children and the empty rawness of grief that was left after the devastation.

"I can't," she whispered, the words barely audible. "It has to stop."

"There's no end to it, child, until we remember who we are." Grandmum Muriel locked her gaze on Catherine's, and with a shudder, fell back on her pillow.

Catherine sat with her until first light, but the old woman never opened her eyes again. Her breathing became increasingly shallow and finally stopped altogether. Catherine sent for her Mum, and they washed the old woman and dressed her in her finest. She was buried in the family plot in the Necropolis. She lay next to her mother Catriona Blair and her grandmother Moira Blair, and Catherine knew her mother would join them one day, and after them, she herself would rest in the same row. She held her mother's hand and watched as the townsfolk laid flowers on the grave. Catherine made a decision as she stood in the rough grass with Mum's hand in hers. She would run the shop, make the lotions and oils, but the rest was to stop. She knew the power it carried and the devastation left in its wake. She was responsible for the souls lost to the rage and anger that night in the field.

Later, as she sat in Mum's kitchen sipping tea and staring at the wall as well-wishers drank glasses of brandy and shared stories about the old woman, Catherine felt the mark on her left wrist pulse in sympathy. I can't, she whispered to it. It has to stop; something so much greater than she, and how was she to control it. Grandmum Muriel couldn't, nor others before her either. The dreams had led her to this, and the only way she knew to combat the weight of the sorrow in her heart was to shut it out entirely. Her life would be ordinary and mundane. She would run the shop, marry a man, have a family, and never again read the rune signs or slam a window shut with a flick of her wrist.

In her cave, the Cailleach felt a tremor and stirred in her deep sleep. She was so close to awakening, and her dreams were becoming more vibrant. She saw the rowan tree where she had last stretched her powers and knew that her many-times great-granddaughter had finally passed to the next life. She would wait a bit longer, but the time was coming and could not be denied for fear or grief.

CHAPTER 43

IT WAS RAINING ON the day that the man knocked on the front door of the manor house on Cathedral Court. It had rained through the night, and Alice was happy to see that the new roof was holding strong. Coira sat in the study at the George IV writing table, meticulously drawing with her charcoal pencil set. She looked tiny and ancient in the big leather office chair. Mum was sitting by the window in the new kitchen, absently drinking tea and staring at the rain. They had been talking about how to handle Coira's primary school. She can wait another year, Mum had said; some children don't start until they're seven even. Alice had sighed. It was true, Coira was only five years old, and she wasn't in any particular hurry to send her off to school every day, but she worried. The little girl was so withdrawn. Wouldn't the company of other children do her some good? Mum had harrumphed and gone back to her tea and staring at the rain. The truth was that Alice had no idea how Coira would handle school. She had never been out of Alice's care; her only babysitter had been Miss Lettie back in England. How would her quiet, intense child handle a room full of rowdy kids? But if she didn't, how much further would she slip into herself?

And then there was the matter of the little everyday occurrences that Alice and Mum had started to take for granted. Coira had made the sugar bowl scoot across the table to her yesterday just by reaching for it. She'd been entirely unfazed, and Alice had had to swallow several times before her voice sounded normal enough to remind Coira that she should ask for it to be passed to her, and to use please and thank you. They had a growing band of stray cats that were collecting at the back door; they cried and yowled until Coira appeared, then the lot of them would walk the grounds together, Coira traipsing off onto the wooded path that led to the cottage. "They did that to you, you know," Mum had said to Alice one day as they watched the little girl setting off on an excursion into the trees with two scabby ginger tabby cats at her heels. Alice had a faint memory of skipping down High Street as a child, delighted at the soft fur of the street cats as they rubbed against her legs and swirled around her feet. "She's good with animals," Alice had said. "That's what we said about you," Mum reminded her.

But today, in the rain, there were no cats, and Coira was quietly tucked away in the study, carefully drawing a scene that looked as though it came half from a nature book of landscapes and half from a nightmare. Alice had held her breath for a minute when she peeked over the girl's shoulder, and then she moved on. The truth was it was a very good drawing, not just good for a five-year-old but good on any scale you applied it to. It was as though a fully grown and educated adult was hiding in the tiny body. If it wasn't for the plush teddy bear sitting opposite the artist, keeping careful watch, one might forget she was a child altogether.

The bell made Alice jump. They rarely had visitors now that the work crews had finished the job, and in the rain it was an entirely foreign sound. Mum looked up, her face confused.

"Who?" she asked simply.

"No idea," Alice said, crossing from the kitchen through the dining room and into the front parlor. The grandeur of the place still made her head swim. She jumped to see Coira standing in the archway that led from the study. The little girl stared at the door, unblinking.

"You forgot to lock it," she said simply.

The bell rang again, insistent. Alice looked at the tidy white front door with the custom trim and realized Coira was right. She had forgotten to lock it; the bolt and the handle were entirely open, and she must have forgotten to do up the lock when she came back in earlier that morning. So few people came anywhere near the house, it wasn't a big concern. The bell rang again. Alice stepped protectively in front of Coira even though she knew the girl was more than capable of taking care of herself. The bell again, followed by a pounding on the door. Alice felt her spine grow cold from the bottom up, spreading into her temples and across her forehead.

Suddenly she saw the path laid out in front of her. She saw the man on the other side of the door. His face was caked with grease from the factories on the other side of town. He had crossed through the Necropolis and into Cathedral Court, but not before he'd hit a few pubs. He was bleary-eyed, unsteady on his feet. He thought he was home; he thought this was the house of the girl he loved, who had kicked him to the streets days ago. He was angry. Alice saw the long knife tucked into the back of his belt. She saw the floor awash in a sea of black-red blood. She saw Mum slumped over the table, her throat slit from ear to ear. She saw herself, splayed against the newly stained dark wood staircase. She heard Coira scream, a long thin sound that seemed to last forever.

"It's okay, Momma," Coira said calmly. "Step back now."

Mum appeared in the opposite archway, sensing the danger as the pounding continued.

"Open up, ya slag!" He was beating with one hand now; the entire door shook with the force. "I know why you tossed me out! I'm home now, ya maggot, and I need to talk to ya!"

"Step back now," Coira repeated, putting her small hand on Alice's arm. "It's okay."

Mum's face was locked in confusion and fear. Alice stepped away from the child she should be protecting, everything in her body telling her to do the opposite. Coira approached the door and laid both hands on it. The pounding stopped completely. Alice steadied herself on the wall as Coira reached to the knob and opened the door. Alice tried to cry out, but she swallowed the sound. The man stood stock-still on the other side as though he had been frozen, and the image of the men in Caracas rushed into Alice's mind. Those men had been unconscious, their eyes closed and their chests moving. This man was a stone: his eyes stared blankly ahead, and no breath escaped his lungs.

"Coira… " Alice began. "Honey… "

Coira turned to look at her, her raven hair with a touch of fire swirling around her face in the wind that escaped into the house, her honey eyes burning with a fire-red tint.

"He killed before he came here, a woman he met in a pub." Coira spoke slowly, as if in a trance. "He took her to a room and slashed her throat. She's there now, no one knows yet. He'll kill after he leaves here, a man who says a harsh word to him. He'll stab him in the gut, and then he will run. The rain will give rise to a fever, and he will die in an alley. His time is over; there's no good left for him to do." Her voice was an intonation, no hint of little girl. She was channeling a far more ancient hag, and she spoke with certainty and with an authority over life and death that was only found in the most ancient of magic.

The little girl turned to face the man who stood still as death in their doorway, his hand raised for the next attack on the door. Coira raised one finger toward his face as though to stroke his cheek; too little to reach his face, she stood on her toes and lightly tapped his chin with her arm fully extended.

The man cracked and shrank, his features becoming something that was not skin, not stone, not bone or wood. It shrank inward and sucked the moisture from the flesh, the cheeks folding in creating a horrid grimace. The eye sockets were two cavernous holes in what had been his face. Mum stood firmly in the archway, her face impassive. Alice felt the mark of Ingwaz on her wrist pulse and throb. The wind whipped madly outside the door, and the rain fell straight down in sheets. The elm and willow trees lining the front of the manor house bent near to breaking. In the midst of the din, the many-greats granddaughter of Cailleach blew a soft breath at the man's face and the form collapsed to ash. The wind swept under the grey matter and spun it into the sky, scattering it in the storm.

The wind calmed, and the rain fell back to a typical Scottish pelt. Coira closed the door and patted down her sodden hair. With a glance at Alice and her grandmum, she trotted back to the study to finish her drawing.

In the black and silent underground lake, a ripple ran slowly and systematically across the still water. The Cailleach lurched to the shore, rubbing her molting skin on the rock as she shuffled along. She ran a single, claw-like finger across the surface of the icy water and lifted it to her face, smelling the sulfur and iron, the certainty of completion that was the promise of Ingwaz. It would come soon.

CHAPTER 44

THE MORNING AFTER THE man had come to their doorstep, the news broke about a young woman found with her throat slashed in Saltmarket. It was said that she'd left a pub with a factory worker, but no one had been able to identify the man. Alice paced the floor while Coira splashed in puddles left by the rain on the land stretching out from the back of the manor.

"There's nothing to report," Mum said firmly. "And who would you tell? You'll end up in the asylum, you will, and that's if they don't laugh you off and ignore it entirely."

Alice knew she was right; there was nothing to be done. They didn't know who the man was, and if Coira was right, and she most definitely was, he would have died that night anyhow but not before taking another life. The little girl had not spoken of the incident since and had slept a full night's sleep. Today she was behaving in an obstinately five-year-old manner, running and jumping into the deepest puddles and then sloshing around.

Alice could see the water seeping over into her galoshes; her feet would be soaked to the bone by now.

Alice rocked against the kitchen counter, her heart pounding in her chest. Behind her, the breakfast dishes rattled and shook in their places, bits of toast and droplets of water dancing out of their containers and onto the table.

"Stop it!" Mum snapped. "Whatever it is you're fretting over is making everything bounce about. You're making a mess."

"A mess?" Alice half laughed, half growled. "A mess? My daughter killed a man yesterday and you're concerned about a mess."

The kitchen cupboards flew open and then slammed shut; a teacup on the edge of the counter fell and shattered on the floor. Alice stood still and looked at the bits of porcelain scattered over dark wood.

"Sit down," Mum ordered.

Alice paused for a moment and then obeyed.

"Do you want to know why I left?" Mum asked, her voice forceful and strict, the tone Alice remembered from her childhood.

"Left here? Glasgow?" Alice asked numbly. "The war. You left because of the war."

"That's what I always told you, wasn't it?" Mum said as she gathered the breakfast plates and stood to place them in the sink. "The war made sense; no one questioned why I would leave a city that had been bloody blasted to hell, where there were still bodies piled in a stack at the graveyard across the way, and we were living off rations of powdered eggs." She slammed a mug of tea in front of Alice and sat back down.

"Mum... why are you telling me this now? I can't even think straight." Alice's mind was racing, as it had been since the news about the girl in Saltmarket had broken. Until then, she had been pretending that what had happened at the front door had been some sort of dream or vision, not literal. Her daughter hadn't really killed a man with the touch of her finger. But for whatever reason, the news about the Saltmarket girl had made it all real.

"You need to know, whether you want to know or not. And given what happened yesterday, there's a serious lack of time." Mum stared at Alice for a moment. "I never taught you about our gift like your Great-Grandmum Muriel did me and your Grandmum Rowan. I never did. I tried to raise you like a normal girl, ordinary in every way, but there were always things we couldn't ignore. That day before we left for Colorado, you nearly drowned, but something saved you. You had spirits watching you all of the time. You walked into a room, and all the air was sucked right out. You traveled with a crowd surrounding you, watching you, telling you things, showing you paths. You were just a child, smaller than Coira even, and I couldn't slow it down, I couldn't stop it." Mum paused, considering her words.

"You don't know the truth I learned about your Great-Grandmum Muriel. And no matter how my Mum tried to explain it all away with her books and science, I know what happened during those days and nights so long ago when the consumption swept through the city." Mum stopped and watched Alice's face for a reaction.

"Mum, TB was everywhere back in those days. Maybe Grandmum Rowan was right and it was just science, nature, inevitable." Alice felt her fingertips growing numb.

"Inevitable, yes. But there was nothing natural about it," Mum said softly. "She brought the illness, spread it through the dirt and water and air. She brought it with the anger and pain that had been inflicted on her. She killed them, Alice; she killed nearly the whole city." Mum leaned in. "I left because I saw what you were becoming capable of and I didn't know how to stop it. I thought that a place where the old magic didn't run so deeply, where we didn't have a history, where you wouldn't remember, might make it stop."

"So what?" Alice asked as the numbness crept up her arms along her veins, heading to her heart. "You think we should leave? That this thing that Coira can do, her oddness, this would all go away if we went somewhere where we can forget?"

"No!" Mum slammed her hands down on the table, her voice filling the room. Alice jumped back and felt the ice-cold numb seek into her neck, chest, lungs.

"No." Mum repeated. "I was wrong to leave. The only way this… " she pulled up her sleeve and indicated the mark of Ingwaz on her wrist, "… this comes to completion is by remembering exactly where we came from and what we are capable of." She pointed at Coira on the great expanse of mud out back. "She is the one who could do that; she could remember and bring this all home for good."

"I don't understand," Alice whispered.

"Neither do I, entirely," Mum answered, her voice gentle now. "Neither of us will ever entirely understand, I suspect. I know this, though: we are a force of nature not unlike that plague of consumption. Our line is that of the ancient hags that used to rule this land, and now we exist in shadows and whispers of our former selves. We have healed and brought life and beauty to this world, but we brought equal measures of death as well. The ancient hags lorded over mankind, guarding them at times and at others striking them down. We were never entirely in this world;

even now, we both have one foot on the other side of the mist. Your daughter... " she indicated Coira, who was kneeling in the sticky mud forming the earth into a shape of some sort. "Your daughter is barely in our world at all. Her physical form is all that keeps her here; her head belongs with the ancient line."

Alice's head was throbbing, the icy numbness making her breath feel like shards of ice. "What do we do?"

Mum shook her head sadly. "That, I don't know," she answered simply and looked out the window at the little girl covered in mud who had a storm of golden dragonflies buzzing around her head. "Only she can answer that. Our job is to wait." Mum paused, her brow furrowing. "Should we stop her? She's an absolute mess."

Alice watched her for a minute and then shook her head. "This is the most like a child she's been in a long while."

Mum smiled softly. "Then let's let her be."

CHAPTER 45

THE YOUNG MAN HAD *come into the shop on an errand from his mother. He wasn't from Glasgow, he said with a broad smile, he'd grown up in Aberdeen. His family though, he said, revealing a row of perfect teeth and a dimple on his left cheek, was from these parts, and his mother had always talked of the shop on High Street. He was a carpenter by trade, come to work in the factories, and would she like to have a pint with him? Catherine turned him down the first time he asked. But the next day he returned, and the day after that, and finally she relented. He asked her about the Girls' Academy, which was still thriving despite the classes getting smaller every year. He asked her why she hadn't gone to university, become a doctor like her mother and father. He stared into her eyes and remembered every word she said, and by the end of the evening, Catherine felt dizzy. He walked her back down High Street and leaned in as she fumbled with the keys to the door. His lips were soft as they brushed hers; he smelled like peppermint and cinnamon.*

He returned every night after his shift at the metal works factory, and she made him dinner, inviting him up to the second-floor flat. Mum and Dad came by to have supper and meet the young man. His eyes were hazel with bits of bright green dancing in them, and Mum asked him a thousand questions about his family, his work, and where he was headed. He smiled, and Catherine saw Mum's crusty exterior melt a bit. Some months later, Mum made a chocolate cake and the neighbors all gathered to toast their nuptials. The wedding was simple, held in the garden of Queen Margaret College underneath the flowering trees as spring bloomed around them. Catherine wore her mother's dress with the lace sleeves and high collar, and her groom borrowed a suit from his dad. They moved into the flat over the shop and led an ordinary life. Catherine took the lessons that Grandmum Muriel had taught her and locked them away. She never explained the truth behind her tiny tattoo and never gave her new husband or family any cause to believe she was anything other than a shopkeeper.

Alice was born the following year on the night of the Autumnal Equinox, the first day of fall, when the leaves grew amber and rust and the birds still sang high in the trees. Catherine lay in bed, cradling her infant daughter and staring into her great, dark eyes. Her hair was raven with a touch of fire, and Catherine swore that she would keep her safe from the secrets she knew. Her daughter would never know the burden of knowledge, never carry the weight of those who had come before her.

The ley lines buzzed in celebration. The ancient line was once again continued, and despite Catherine's proclamation, the Cailleach stretched an ancient hand into the void and ran it back over her matted hair. A great black clod of molt fell from her scalp, and she lifted the mass to her lips, tasting the salty coarseness of the shreds of her humanity. The hag would need to wait years, but after thousands, a few more were no matter. Each child born remembered a bit more and gained a bit more strength. Eventually, there would come a child who would grow and remember, and the line would come full circle. Farther away, in her cabin on the cliff side, the raven-haired hag looked up from her work; she felt the vibration of the ley lines as well and knew the time was coming when the line of daughters that had been lost to the world of man for so long would cross back over the Lethe and bring with them the wisdom of the ages.

CHAPTER 46

"DID I EVER TELL you about my hat?" Alice asked her honey-eyed daughter as she tucked the rose-colored quilt up to her neck and slipped her ragged teddy bear to her side.

Coira shook her head and hugged her bear to her chest.

"Would you like to know?" Alice asked softly, brushing her raven hair back from her forehead. The child nodded and stared at her with eyes that had grown far too old in far too little a time.

"When I was just a girl, not too much older than you, really, we had just moved to the United States, and we didn't live in Grandmum's cabin in the woods yet, and I was lonely. I didn't have any friends, and I think Grandmum worried a bit about me. She put me in a dance class. Tap dance was what it was called, and I was rather good at it, if I do say so myself." Alice smiled at her daughter's solemn face that soaked in everything she said with such intensity.

"I had a particular costume that I was so very proud of, and it had a silly top hat—black silk with a neat little bow around the rim. I printed my name in it so no one could ever walk away with it and say it was theirs. 'Alice Grace Kyles' it said, printed there in ink with my own hand. A couple of years later, we were all moving up to the woods—Grandmum, your Great-Aunt Polly, your Uncle Arthur who you never got a chance to meet but you would have loved so very much. The four of us were moving to the cabin and were throwing out all our rubbish and packing our bags. I found my old hat in a box, and your Grandmum asked me if I wanted to keep it, but I said no. It didn't fit any more by then, you see, and I wasn't taking the dance class any more, so I threw it in the trash and I thought it was gone forever.

"I never saw it again until over ten years later. Your father showed up at my door with that crazy hat in his hands. I thought I had gone mad to see him standing there, his ginger hair hanging in his face, silly grin on his lips, holding that hat. He told me it had nearly killed him, and did I want it back? I think I told him to go away and put it back in the trash where it belonged. But he didn't go away. Instead he told me how he had been driving up Ute Pass, and he was behind a truck full of old rubbish, old furniture, and boxes of records and whatnot. Then, as he was driving, a box blew open as though something had jumped inside it, and that hat came flying out. The way your father told it, it sailed straight into the air and then straight back down and fixed itself right onto his windshield. He nearly drove right off the road. When he did stop, he had to tug it off the car as though it were stuck with glue, and that's when he saw my name printed in the lining. Alice Grace Kyles."

Coira smiled, and the rarity of the expression on her stoic face made Alice's heart warm.

"He knew me, you see, and he thought I'd never speak to him, but here was this hat, like a sign."

"You loved him," Coira said simply.

"In my way, I did. He was not easy to love, but as he stood there in my doorway, so young, I saw his path, and I saw you, and I knew that no matter where it took me, I had to follow. So, yes, I suppose I did love him." Alice's throat tightened, and she ran a finger down Coira's soft cheek.

"He understands," Coira said softly. "He told me that the world was a loud place when he was living, so many voices and sounds, and it was so confusing for him. Now he can see clearly, and it's quiet."

"You talk to him?" Alice asked, not wanting to push too far.

"A bit," Coira said with a little shrug. "But he hadn't told me about the hat. I like that story."

With that, she rolled over, hugging her plush bear, and closed her eyes. Alice kissed her forehead and turned off the lamp, leaving the little girl to her dreams and the moonlight.

CHAPTER 47

ALICE GRACE KYLES WAS *two years old. She did not understand why Mum was so very angry and why Dad's voice was raised so very loudly and why Mum had slapped her hand away from the little green plant in the courtyard garden and why she had been sent up here to her room when she was hungry for her tea. All she could do was cry and bury her tiny head in her worn pillow.*

In the shop below, Catherine paced the floor.

"I don't understand why you're so upset. She didn't mean to kill the plant; she must have poured something in it. She's a child, for god's sake." Catherine's hazel-eyed husband was entirely confused by her reaction, and there was no way she could explain what it was that had upset her so.

The child had been wandering to and fro in the courtyard, as she tended to do. As Catherine watched, she reached a tiny hand out to a sprig of peppermint growing in a row along the window. At the same moment, a bee that had landed on the girl's bare arm stung her, and the child cried in pain. Catherine rushed to her but stopped in her tracks to see the peppermint, still intertwined in the child's fingers, turn to ash and blow away in the summer breeze. A chill ran from the top of Catherine's head to her toes, and she slapped the girl's hands away from the window box. The little girl, her arm aching from the bee sting and her eyes wide with surprise, screamed in confusion and pain. When Catherine's husband came home, she had tried to explain that the child had been messing about in the garden and that was why she was being punished. It didn't make any sense, and no one but Catherine knew exactly what it meant.

Mum had already warned her about Alice's unconscious abilities. Mum had seen the child sit perfectly still in the courtyard and the next minute be covered in a dozen bright butterflies. They swirled and danced around her and then flew away while the girl giggled. Alice had no conscious awareness of the things she could do, and so far her father had not seen a thing out of the ordinary. She's good with animals, he said blindly when the skittish street cats followed her down the lane or the bluebirds landed on her picnic blanket and ate from her hand. She has your talent, he said with his eyes flashing bits of green in the hazel, as the child revived a drooping flower with the touch of her hand. Each incident left Catherine feeling queasy and unsettled.

Did you know? Catherine asked her Mum in regard to Grandmum Muriel one night as her family slept upstairs and they sat over cups of thick black tea in the tiny shop. Did you know about Grandmum Muriel?

I knew she was attacked by a group of men in the woods, Mum answered. I knew she was never the same and that was how I was conceived. I knew I was born in the midst of a wave of consumption that nearly wiped out the city. I knew that was probably a bit of why I was driven to study medicine. I have always known that all the women in our family are extraordinary and you more than most. I knew that, no matter how I tried to conceal my part in our family's unique talents, she said with a small smile. I knew that even I could not entirely hide behind my books and labs. Your daughter will not be able to hide much longer either, and as the women in our family have done for ages, you have to teach her, guide her.

But Mum, Catherine pleaded. I can't, she cried.

Your Grandmum didn't usher in anything that wasn't already headed this way, Mum said softly. Our line is ancient and based in something far older than man or nature. Nature is cruel; illness sweeps through a city and pays no never-mind to who is innocent or guilty. You cannot blame your Grandmum for a force that is far older than even our line. Plague, disease, illness—it sits just below the surface of our cities and fields; it waits for us to look away and forget the danger we're in. Whatever transpired in that field on that terrible day so long ago, you cannot use it to deny your daughter her gifts.

Catherine heard her mother's voice but still could not erase the image of the rowan tree falling to ash and the burning of blood as it rose from her lungs to her lips. She shook her head. Her daughter would have a chance at an ordinary life, free from the ancient burden that followed her and all the women that had come before.

CHAPTER 48

ARTHUR JAMES KYLES WAS *born in a caul like his aunt. And like his aunt, he was born blue and still, unbreathing and motionless. Catherine, near unconscious from the blood loss and exhaustion, had known something was wrong for weeks; nothing terribly obvious, just a growing dread, and then the cramping and pain had started. The bombing raids that rocked the walls and filled the air with ash and smoke had been incessant, and Mum, in her fear, had moved Catherine to the hospital at Queen Margaret's and Alice to the cottage on the lot of land behind the manor house on Cathedral Court. It was on the far end of town, away from the munitions factory, and had escaped much of the destruction wrought upon the rest of Glasgow. Catherine's green-eyed husband was three months gone with the 15th Infantry Division. Last she had heard, he was outside London, but the mail took an age to pass back and forth so he could be anywhere by now. There had been no way to tell him the baby was coming, and for all Catherine knew, he could be dead already.*

The nurses were rushing back and forth, a neatly bearded doctor was calmly issuing orders, and Catherine felt a weight on her chest that made it impossible to breathe. Alice and her grandfather were in the next room, waiting. Alice, barely out of toddling, was old enough to understand that it was too early for the baby. Mum was right there by the bedside, allowed only because she was a senior member of the medical school faculty and would not take no for an answer. The pain was unbearable until finally the baby boy was pulled from inside her, his tiny body unwilling to make the journey on its own. Later, Catherine would say it was as though he knew he was entering a world that had fallen to the darkest parts of itself. A world shaken by the continual roar of machines from the sky, the constant threat of death and fire; it was a world that had been flipped upside down to expose the ugliness and evil that had previously lain dormant. Catherine did not fault her baby boy for not wanting to enter such a world.

The room was oddly still as the infant's limp body met the Scottish air for the first time. A hush fell over the nurses, and even the stoic doctor sat perfectly still for a moment before barking out more orders. The baby lay still on the little metal table, where the doctor pressed his tiny chest and listened for a heartbeat while the nurses fluttered nervously around, tending to Catherine and hovering over the doctor's shoulders. Finally, Mum couldn't take it any more.

"Give him to us, just give him to us," she ordered. The nurses looked to the doctor, who gave a small nod and a look of deepest sympathy to Catherine. The baby was dead, stillborn, and nothing could be done. The nurses wrapped the tiny creature in a blanket and laid him on Catherine's chest.

"Let us have a moment with him," Mum said quietly to the doctors and nurses, who filed out, exhausted and defeated. Mum made sure the door was shut and the room empty before crossing back to Catherine, who was stroking the tiny, still face and weeping softly.

"None of that," Mum said briskly. "You know what to do. I know your Grandmum taught you well."

Catherine shook her head slightly. She couldn't, she had left that behind, she had a normal life now, even Alice's uncanny incidences had slowed. They were normal people, and this tragedy was, in all its horror, what nature intended.

"You don't have much time. His soul is still here waiting for you to call it back," Mum said, her voice firm. "You know the words, you have to do it. You're his mother."

Catherine looked down at the tiny being, his perfect, miniature fingers and delicate ears. A son, rare in their line; a miracle she had never expected. His tiny lips were parted slightly, and his body was growing cold. He'd never drawn a breath, he would never open his eyes. She would never know if he had his father's hazel or her family's darkness. The few scraps of hair on his head were tawny, lighter than any of Catherine's line, fiery and fierce.

"You have to do it, or he will die," Mum said softly. "He is waiting for you to call him back. Only you can speak the words, only you can bring him back, and you must do it now or he will be lost to this world forever."

Catherine swallowed a sob; he was perfectly formed, tiny angular nose and long eyelashes. But what world was she bringing him into? A world where the rumble of explosions and destruction lasted through the night and into the dawn? A world where the bodies of children were pulled from the rubble, and hundreds walked the streets, huddling in corners and alleyways, their homes destroyed. She felt her mother's hand on her shoulder and closed her eyes, the symbol of Ingwaz dancing behind her eyelids. The certainty of a conclusion; that was what the rune meant—the idea that for every start, there was a purpose. Catherine opened her eyes, and with all the remaining strength she had, begged the universe and all the goddesses and gods to tell her what to do. Was she to save a life that would be lost to a bloody and painful death? Outside the hospital walls, a rumble shook the sky, and Catherine looked up to lock eyes with her mother. Her mother, who had seen countless horrors in war already and came out on the other side. Her mother who had defied every expectation; her mother who had once brought an infant lost to a caul back to life.

Catherine leaned to whisper the ancient words in the infant's ear. She felt the mark on her wrist pulse in time with each syllable. The language was as rough as the lowland crags and unrecognizable to all but the most ancient of hags. She felt a tingling sensation rush through her body, and her head felt disconnected from her neck. The words came out on their own as they slipped into the current. This was the way Grandmum Muriel had told her; this was the magic that was lying dormant in her soul, always waiting for a key to open the door. All this was poured into the infant boy's ear and flowed through his veins and into his tiny, immobile heart. With a gasp, he opened his eyes and regarded his mother with a solemn, dark stare. His tiny fingers wriggled, and he looked at them as though amazed. Mum knelt down and laid a hand on both of them, and Catherine felt a flow of energy pulse through their hands. His lips lost their blue hue and opened wide. His scream made Catherine weep, the sobs uncontrolled and full of shock and joy.

The door flew open, and the doctor stood there, his mask pulled down onto his chin and his eyes wide.

"He woke up," Mum said with a satisfied tone.

Later, as Alice slept in a cot in the corner of the hospital room, Catherine sat in her hospital bed holding her baby boy. There was a part of his chest that still held the grey-blue rot that he had been born with. She knew that for the miracle that he was, she was too late. Death had sunk a claw into him while she waited and agonized. She held him closer, stroking his sleeping cheek, now pink and warm. She shivered to feel the power that had coursed through her and Mum's hands, and how, like Polly so many years before, it had defied nature.

CHAPTER 49

THE BACK LAWN, SODDEN from the rains, was now peppered with dozens of mounds of mud and dirt. Alice watched Coira from a wicker rocking chair on the back patio. She hadn't said a word while her daughter worked from the time the sun came up to when it fell in the sky. She had marched out into the dawn light wearing a pair of trousers, her raincoat, and galoshes. Methodically and with great care, she had knelt in the muddy and sodden field, gathering up handfuls of sticky clay and forming them into oblong shapes that rose from the earth. The tallest among them stood to Coira's knees, the shortest just above her ankle. Alice couldn't see from here, but they appeared to have details that Coira had carved into them, almost like features on a human face. When she finished one, she moved on to another.

It was remarkable, Alice thought as she rocked and observed. By all rights, they should collapse and crumble once they dried, but instead, even the tallest of the lot seemed to have hardened into a form of clay even though the meager sun brought little heat. The rain had staved, despite what was predicted, and Alice couldn't help but wonder if the little girl out in the field, covered in mud and grime, had had anything to do with that. The summer solstice was coming up soon, the longest day of the year, but the Scottish weather felt far from summery.

Alice closed her eyes and tried to make sense of the dream she had had last night. She had been on a rocky shore. A high sea cliff rose from the sand upward to land overlooking the water. To her right was a small fishing village with wooden cottages and planks laid side by side for walkways. A great wooden dock stood in the water, and ships were lined up and down in the port. There was no sign of life or any movement but for the light of a small candle flickering in the window of one small cottage. Alice had crossed the plank walkway to the rough-hewn door and knocked. She felt no fear or cold; the moon hung high and illuminated the scene as though it were day. The door swung open at her touch, and Alice saw a woman sitting in a worn wooden chair in front of a dead fireplace. The woman turned to regard Alice as she entered. Her face was covered with a cross pattern of lines and sags. Her scalp was bare but for a few long strands of fire-red hair that fell haphazardly like a spider's web. Her eyes were huge and dark, and they stared at Alice as she stood in the doorway.

"You'll be wanting to see my mother, I expect." The figure spoke without moving her lips, the sound reverberating through Alice's head. She lifted one bony finger to point up, up to the sea cliffs. As she pointed, Alice could see the symbol on her left wrist, the intersecting jagged lines of Ingwaz.

"Go on now." With that, the hag turned to face the dead, black fireplace again. Alice tried to speak, but her throat was caught;

no sound escaped, no breath. She backed out of the cottage and looked up at the cliffside. She could see a faint light, no brighter than a candle, far, far on the very top. As she stared, the water on the shore was sucked back into the ocean. With a thunderous roar, it reared up far into the sky and lurched forward, alien tendrils of sea water clawing their way to the top of the rocky cliff. As Alice watched, it hung in midair for a still moment: the moment before everything ended, before nothing could ever be ordinary again. It hung with spits of icy seawater escaping to the wind and blowing to and fro. It hung as though a great hand with a set of strings hovered above it.

Then, with a deafening crash, it fell onto the town. Alice saw the wooden structures and the port split and fly apart. Just as the water reached her toes, Alice snapped awake. She lay in bed, breathing heavily and trying to persuade her heart to stop pounding. Just then, from the corner of her bedroom with the little window seat, she heard a voice.

"I love this room," it said in a thin and wistful tone. "I kept a piano and a harp in here. Never learned to play much, mind you."

Alice shot up in bed and saw a woman not much older than her sitting on the forest-green cushions that lined the window seat. Her raven-fire hair, so much like Alice's, was swept up in an elaborate series of twists and turns. Her eyes were huge and dark. Her body melted into the moonlight, giving the impression that she was as inconsistent as the breeze.

"It's time to go. The girl is waiting for you to understand. Time is coming soon." The woman spoke gently, the sound filling Alice's head and dancing from one ear to the other before fading away like a wisp of smoke. She lifted her left hand and pointed up. As she did so, Alice could see the mark of Ingwaz glowing on her moonlit skin.

Alice fought her body, willing it to rise, to move, to cross to the figure in the window. But her body lay still and her muscles betrayed her intent. I'm still asleep, Alice realized with a shock. I'm still dreaming; my body is asleep. She tried to scream, but her voice was frozen solid. In the midst of the struggle, she felt the darkness overtake her, and she fell back into an inky star-filled sky.

The next time Alice awoke, light was seeping through the curtains, and she knew her body was entirely hers again. She wouldn't tell Mum or Coira about her dream; she needed to figure it out for herself first. Coira's birthday was coming soon, right as the seasons turned to summer. Alice wondered what this year would bring. Coira would soon be the same age she had been when she'd left Glasgow as a child. She felt a sense of urgency, and a vision of the seaside cliffs from her dream flashed behind her eyes. It was time to wake up and lead her daughter to whatever was to come next.

CHAPTER 50

COIRA ONLY CAME INSIDE after the sun had fallen and the night wind had begun to whip through the trees. She hadn't eaten all day; all attempts to offer food or rest had been refused. She was entranced with her singular and utterly mysterious task, and her work caught the light of the rising moon. Mum lifted her off the ground as soon as she hit the doorway and carried her to the bath. The little girl sat impassively as her grandmum scrubbed the dirt and mud off her hands and face.

Alice watched from the doorway. Time had started to escalate and move faster; she could feel her blood beating in a higher pulse than before. Once Coira was clean and dry, they sat her down to a steak and kidney pie at the kitchen table. She ate slowly; once finished, she neatly folded her napkin and walked to the front room. There she stood, gazing out at the stone steps and willows in the front of the manor. Alice came to stand behind her. If you looked just beyond the edges of Cathedral Court, you could see the Necropolis, where generations of their line lay.

"What else did you see?" Coira asked quietly.

Alice flinched these were the first words she had spoken all day. The little girl looked more ghost than child, standing there in the moonlight that poured through the big front window in her gauzy, white nightgown.

"That day on the lane, when you were a little girl, you saw my father, and you saw me, and you saw how he would die. But what else did you see?" The little girl's voice had lost all childishness; it was smooth and velvet, like a chant.

"I didn't understand the other things I saw that day," Alice answered honestly. "I still don't. I only knew that it was the conclusion to a long story—that it was everything that Ingwaz represents, the certainty of a conclusion, a bringing of peace and a healing of the past with the present."

"Yes, but what did you see?" Coira turned to face her mother. Her eyes caught the light of the candle on the wall sconce, and they glowed amber, luminescent in the light. "Tell me the things you saw."

Alice felt the numbness tingling in her fingertips again. "I saw shapes of people, shadows half-formed, the light bleeding through them. I saw them everywhere: they stood on corners and streets; they looked out the windows of the lane where I lived. They were children and women and men; they were lost. I saw you, as you are right now, and I knew it was near the solstice. I saw them all coming home."

Coira paused, considering all this. Then she turned and continued to stare out the window at the street below. "Yes," she said quietly. "That is what I saw too."

That night, after Coira had finally consented to sleep, Alice lay in her bed, her head pulsing. The solstice would be here soon, only days away, and it would bring the wave she had seen in her dream, the wave that washed away what was and cleansed the shore. She felt sleep tugging her under, and soon she was drifting on the inky black starlit sky.

She stood high on the sea cliff. Below, the ocean crashed and raged; the rough field grass bit and cut her feet as she walked to a tiny cabin with a trail of smoke emanating from the chimney. As she stepped closer to the cabin, she felt as though she had passed through a wall of water although her hair and skin were dry. Her breath was caught in her throat for a moment and she gasped for air. Once through, she walked on to the door, which swung open as she approached.

A woman sat at a dark wood table in front of the crackling hearth. Alice was suddenly shivering violently. With an effortless wave of her long, delicate fingers, the woman beckoned her in. Alice entered and sat next to the creature. It was not a woman in the human sense, though she was undeniably beautiful. Her raven hair fell around her face, which, while unlined and olive-toned, was not quite mortal. Her features were too sharp; her night-black eyes reflected the starry night sky. She held out her left wrist, showing the mark of Ingwaz. Alice stared at her, mesmerized.

In front of the woman was a small stack of squares of muslin cloth; beside them, a bottle of indigo ink. Alice had seen her mother try to recreate the image for Coira, but now she knew why she had said it was not enough: the air around the cloth and ink sparked and crackled. Wordlessly, the woman dropped a pinpoint of indigo ink onto the stack of cloth, and it sank down layer after layer after layer. Alice reeled back, the truth overwhelming her and knocking her to the floor. The woman pushed back her chair and lay down next to her, her hand on Alice's heart, the fire warm and comforting, and Alice remembered.

She walked across the heath that the daughter of Cailleach had crossed. She felt the rough field grass shredding her feet and legs. She walked on although her body ached and her heart was in pieces. She felt the cruelty of the children, the sharp blows of the stones, the lick of the flames. She felt a desperate and deep longing for her mother, and Ingwaz pulsed and sang in tune with her grief. Alice walked and the stars swirled above her. Time did not exist here; she was crossing between the layers of the cloth, she was the pinpoint of indigo ink, she knew all things and was equally present in all times. The entrance to the cave glowed in the night, Ingwaz carved on the stones that were pulled back from the entrance.

She entered the pure blackness without fear. Fear was far beyond her now. She was one of an ancient line of hags who had once ruled this land; there was nothing she feared. Down, down, down she went, one foot in front of the other, waiting to feel her mother's arms around her, waiting to feel the comfort of home.

The waters of the black lake far beneath the surface of the lowland crags rippled, and the motion sent gentle waves to lap the shore. The Cailleach turned to see her daughter, her face not mortal and not human; she appeared as she had appeared to the villagers and farmers back in the beginning, as she had to the men she took to amuse herself. Her fire-red hair swirled around her, and her amber dark eyes glowed. She opened her arms to the girl who stood at the door to her home and folded her in. Alice watched all this from the comfort of the inky black sky that had absorbed her as she entered the cavern. It was not she who the Cailleach was folding into her embrace, it was a little girl with raven-fire hair and honey eyes. A little girl whose path Alice had seen all those years ago standing on High Street. A little girl who would bring the certainty of a conclusion, the unity of Ingwaz, and a time of infinite peace to the world of man.

CHAPTER 51

THE LAST LETTER CATHERINE'S *hazel-eyed husband wrote was brief and nonsensical. There was no accompanying explanation for its brevity or oddness, but she imagined that he had had very little time to write it and a certainty that he would not live through the night. It had been found on his body and sent on later; hence, it arrived a week after she received the telegram stating that he had been killed in a bombing raid in London. The telegram did not tell Catherine what she found out later, which was that he had been crushed under the wall of a tenement building where his unit had been rescuing survivors of the Blitz. He died alongside three others from his unit and was hailed as a hero for his bravery. His last note, handwritten in faint pencil and stained with sweat and grease, said nothing of bravery; it spoke of fear, which, Catherine mused, is a sort of bravery in itself, the inception of bravery, a seed that must grow if it is to become useful. And maybe, in time, that fear would have sprung wings and evolved into a much greater thing. But, as it was, the note was scared and sad and lonely, and Catherine could only stand to read it once, folding it tightly and fitting it into a locket she wore around her neck, a grainy photo of her hazel-eyed husband accompanying it.*

They were still staying with Mum and Dad. High Street had escaped the raids thus far, but the threat was always looming. On this day, Catherine had left the children with Mum and made a trip back to her shop with the flat overhead, which was largely untouched but for some broken glass as jars had been shaken from their shelves. No one had broken in, and she hadn't expected they would. Most of High and Bell streets were abandoned, and anyone who had the option had left after the destruction at Clydebank. Mum and Dad had been some of the first doctors to arrive with the Red Cross Brigade, and Mum still wouldn't talk of what she had seen. Dad had sat quietly, chewing on an unlit pipe and staring. Catherine knew better than to ask, but from the stories that swirled, hundreds had died, countless more left homeless. The only detail of that night that Mum would tell Catherine was the body of a small girl who was pulled from the destruction. The bombers were still raging overhead, aiming for the munitions plant and not caring what they brought down in their wake. The girl, even in death, had a fierce grip on a plush tiger—a nervous response, Mum had muttered, the muscles lock into place at the time of death. She was missing a leg and the back of her head was crushed, but her hand was still locked on the tiger. The bodies were piled and the survivors evacuated. Mum had been working around the clock at Queen Margaret's, and her face was gaunt and drawn.

Catherine had walked around the shop, eventually going upstairs and gathering a few things: a doll that Alice had left behind, a blanket, some clothes left in the closet. Her hazel-eyed husband's presence in the flat was still strong. His tea mug still sat on the shelf, ready to be filled; his shirts hung neatly side by side, waiting to be worn. A pair of work boots was lined up by the door, where they had been on the day he left in his clean and pressed uniform. He hadn't said goodbye on that last day; he made a foolish joke, and Catherine had felt nonplussed. It was as though he were off for a holiday at the shore; he refused to talk about the possibility that he might not return. Catherine stood in the doorway to their bedroom and could still see him standing in front of the wooden vanity, straightening his tie and smoothing the wrinkles out of his uniform. He had spent all of his working life in the iron works factory, and the British Army uniform was the first set of dress clothes he'd ever owned. He'd looked so handsome; it had made Catherine's heart flutter.

Alice was now old enough for Primary School—if it had still been open. The war had meant the end of so many things, so Alice was home with her Grandmum and Granddad reading from an aged copy of Gray's and being forced to memorize the periodic table. She had read early; in fact, Catherine couldn't remember when Alice couldn't read. No one had ever taught her that Catherine could remember; it was as though she'd always known, born with the knowledge and practice. When Catherine bent down to tell her the news about her father, her tiny perfect face was grave. She had nodded and not cried, and then turned and crossed to Mum's courtyard, where she sat under the eaves for the rest of the afternoon. Storm clouds rolled in, and it rained for three solid days even though it was the dry season. The neighbors all exclaimed about the odd weather, but Catherine was far from surprised.

Arthur would have no working memories of his father. He had never met him and would have to learn about him through photographs and stories. A ghost before he developed a working memory; Catherine wondered what sort of man that would make him. She wondered how he existed at all. It wasn't unheard of for her line to have sons. Mum had talked of Many-Greats Grandmum Moira and her brothers, and there were male names scratched into the sides of the family Bible who had fallen even before that. It was rare, though, and had not occurred for quite some time. Little Arthur was small for his age. He was one year old and should have been pulling himself up on everything and getting into a grand mess, as Alice had at that age, but he barely crawled. Instead, he rolled and wiggled to where he wanted to be, and when he arrived, wheezed and panted to catch his breath. Mum had taken him to the hospital, where they'd attached the little boy to all manner of breathing machines to measure his lung capacity and tried nebulizers to control his shortness of breath. There was no formal diagnosis that the doctors could make for Arthur's condition. Both Mum and Catherine knew the cause and knew just as well that there was no cure. He had never been meant for this world; an ancient magic had brought him back, and that came with a price.

Polly, the other baby who was never meant to be, had paid her own price. She was safe from the bombings and violence of Britain, but her husband with the ridiculous mustache had enlisted with the American Air Force and been shot down over Germany. There was no confirmation of his death and no reason to believe he was alive. Polly wrote often; she wanted Catherine to come to Colorado, United States, and join her. It was peaceful here, she wrote. No bombings; children played in the street; they rode bicycles and climbed trees without the threat of death. Catherine could read the subtext, however; Polly was alone and scared. Her heart was broken, and she was far from everything she had ever known. Catherine ached for her—her little sister whom she had protected like a lion throughout their youth. Polly had been small like Arthur; the caul had taken its pound of flesh for her revival. She didn't even quite reach five feet tall and was thin as a wisp. No one believed she was grown, and it had been Catherine's job, all the way up until the time when her man with the ridiculous mustache had swept in, to make sure that her little sister, never meant for this world, was safe from the darkness of it.

Catherine left the little shop with the flat overhead, locking the door. Her heart was in pieces. She longed for the simple days so long ago when she'd shared this sacred space with Grandmum Muriel, the licorice smell of the old woman's hair, and her tea that would hold a spoon upright in its cup. She remembered the sweet days when she'd lived here alone, the space entirely hers—hers and the spirits of Grandmum Muriel and Great-Grandmum Catriona. She felt them every day at that time, but they never intruded. They watched and listened and waited. She remembered her hazel-eyed husband, so gobsmacked that a woman could have her own business and live alone. The first time he'd sat at her table for a meal, his face smeared with grease from the iron works, it was as if he'd entered a chapel and seen Jesus himself when she served him a fresh meat pie from the oven. She remembered the way his lips had lingered on hers and the confounding smell of cinnamon and cloves that saturated his skin. She remembered the way his hands moved over her body and how she had moved in rhythm with him. Catherine stood on the cobblestone of High Street and looked up at the second-floor window and remembered Alice, learning to walk, grabbing everything in sight, knocking over more than she captured. They had laughed. She'd been happy here, but she sensed the time for this place was ending. The ink on her left wrist pulsed, and she felt a shift in the wind.

Far across the lowland crags, the Cailleach blew a gentle breeze from her fingertips. In the darkness of the cave, she saw a voyage for her many-greats granddaughter, a trip that would take her farther than any of their line had gone before. She felt the movement of the ocean beneath her and the spirits of her many granddaughters swirl around her in preparation. She would leave this place to discover what she had already known: the promise of completion, the intertwining of the jagged lines, and a whole made from the collected parts of the many. She closed her eyes and rested. The Lethe would be crossed soon, but for now she slept and waited.

CHAPTER 52

ON THAT FIRST DAY of summer, a light rain was falling and the three hags, the many-greats granddaughters of Cailleach, sat huddled in the parlor of the great manor house watching the grey sky and waiting. Alice knew only what she had seen in her dream, and Coira hadn't spoken in days. She drew with her charcoal pencils; once an image was finished, she put it aside and started another. They were images of Glasgow, the inconsistent and ghostly beings that Alice had seen in her vision so very long ago. They stood on street corners waiting for a carriage to pass; they stared at the viewer as though they knew it was almost time. A woman, her hair catching the light and disappearing into the shadows, leaned from a window on the narrow lane off High Street, her face impassive. She had been waiting a long time to come home.

Coira sat on the floor between the two women drawing the domed headstones and granite crosses of the Necropolis. Alice and Mum hadn't moved except to fill the three tea mugs and collect more blankets. A cold draft filled the house, and Alice knew it had nothing to do with the dank weather outside. The wave was rearing up, collecting weight and speed; soon it would crash, and this life they had fought for and nearly accepted as their own would soon be past. The certainty of a conclusion; the end of a line.

Alice felt a strange sort of melancholy. She remembered her little girl, just a year or so ago, giggling over a book of corgis of the Royal Family. She remembered how she would slowly and deliberately climb the stairs at Miss Lettie's; too young to accomplish the task on her own, she did anyway, one tiny foot at a time, Alice holding her breath with each movement the little girl made, her worry all for naught as the child had always been beyond her protection. Alice remembered the day she'd been born; the cramps and pain had started in the early morning hours, and Miss Lettie had set about getting the hospital bag in the car, and Paul had fretted and fussed, pacing back and forth, trying to offer her an arm to hold while going down the stairs.

And then the most amazing thing had happened: the car wouldn't start. No reason for it. The ignition clicked and clicked and nothing happened. Miss Lettie had pitched a fit, demanding that the hospital send a bus immediately, but Alice had known there wasn't time. Coira had entered the world in the sanctuary of Alice's second-floor bedroom, her refuge from the confusion and stress of that time. By the time the medics pulled up in the driveway, Alice had her baby daughter with the honey eyes wrapped in a knit blanket and settled on her chest. Even in infancy, there was nothing the baby girl needed from the world of man.

The light outside the window shifted, and Alice knew that soon the wave would fall, destroying everything they knew. The ink would sink to the next layer, as would they. The world around them already seemed less coherent, as though the seams and edges were starting to blur. Beside her, Mum reached over and took her hand, and Alice squeezed back. Coira looked up from her charcoal pencil and paper.

"Hello," she said simply.

Alice blinked to see shadowy figures moving from the edges of the light into the room. They all shared the raven-fire hair and great dark eyes. They all appeared as they had at their peak of power and strength. Alice gasped to see Grandmum Rowan, her hair loose and free, her eyes unlined, a sad, sweet smile on her face. She entered from a haze of the departing daylight and crossed to kneel next to Coira. The little girl smiled and gave a small nod. The figure from the bedroom that had spoken to Alice, her hair pulled up in elaborate twists and turns, knelt beside her, and Alice looked into the eyes of her Many-Greats Grandmum Moira, who had built this house and been responsible for their lives in Glasgow. Others arrived, and Mum gasped to see Grandmum Muriel, her hair more fire than raven, her eyes bright and free. Others gathered too: Catriona and Muireall, dressed in the indigo robes of the order of women who had taught her the secrets of the hills and land. The shadows grew as the light faded, and still more appeared: a girl with fire hair who had lived her life in a fishing village and shared her name with the child who sat calmly at the center of the shadows and light. A breeze that smelled of heather and burdock filled the room, and the raven-haired hag who had sat at the top of the seaside cliffs and watched man for centuries was finally among them.

She nodded at Coira, who sat calmly and still in the midst of the dying light. Outside the windows, the light began to flicker. Alice turned to see the masses of dried mud and clay begin to grow and change. She gasped as the earth stretched and formed limbs, torsos, eyes, and skin. The earth and clay fell away from their newly formed legs as one by one they began to march across the sodden grass toward the house, the first rain of the summer washing the dirt and mud from their mouths and noses. As they approached, they caught the last bits of daylight—and, like a piece of refracted glass, the light danced in rainbows across the parlor. Alice realized that she had been holding her breath, and as she let it go, she saw the faces of the women and men from the charcoal drawings at the window, newly formed from balls of clay like the first man in the old stories.

"It's time now," Coira said, and the centuries of hags that filled the room collectively looked to the child, who raised her hand in front of her and opened the door.

"Come," she whispered, and the insubstantial forms began to file into the room, kneeling before Coira, one after another after another. Alice sank to the floor and wrapped her arms around her little girl, who turned to face her with an unreadable smile on her small face.

"You've led us here," Coira said, "and now I must take us home. This is the completion of our line, and with it we take the souls of those who died in war and pain, the ones who starved to death and died of disease, those who died at the hands of men in violence and fear. With it we take that scar from this world and leave it afresh. We cleanse the sorrow and misery from this place. We give them a chance to start over. " Coira looked at the growing crowd that filled the parlor and into the hall. Outside the light rain began to pelt the earth, washing away the last of the dirt and clay from the women and men who filled the house, who had come here to follow Coira home.

Low rumbles of thunder rolled across the sky, shaking the house. Overhead, Moira's crystal chandelier rocked back and forth. The rain beat harder, and Alice knew the wave was beginning to fall. They were ready, and there was no fear or sadness; the circle had been completed and with it a chance for peace in this small corner of the world. The intersecting lines of Ingwaz hummed in harmony, and the many daughters of Cailleach remembered their lives and fates. The Lethe had been crossed, and the storm outside the great manor house raged and fought the shift in the wind. A great crack of lightning flashed across the sky, illuminating the souls inside the house. A window shattered, spraying glass and drops of rain and wind.

The drop of indigo ink reached the last square of muslin cloth, and the Cailleach stepped from her cave, arms outstretched. The ley lines fired across the earth and traveled straight to the manor house on Cathedral Court. The floors shook with the weight of the centuries, and the ancient line of hags became one with the torrential Scottish wind, leaving behind their mortal forms as they flew out the manor house, through the ancient streets of Glasgow and further still, across the rough lowland grass, across the night, letting the unearthly glow of the stars overhead be their guide, leading the souls of the lost home to the underground lake set deep below the lowland crags. Coira paused at the entrance to the cave, the great stones with the ancient rune symbols moving into place. No one would find this place until the ancient line of hags was ready to rise again. The Cailleach closed her eyes in a final rest, and the one who was no longer a child, no longer bound by time or age, took her place at the edge of the underground lake. The hags of Cailleach traveled far across the waters to the place that lay beyond, but Coira would wait. Every passing generation or so, she took a man to be her mate. Her ageless soul appeared as an intoxicating blur of raven-fire hair and honey eyes. Her mate would father a child, and together they would live in the enchanted caves behind the rune stones until he died of old age or she tired of his company and set him back on the road, the memory of the time he'd spent in the cave a blind spot in his mind.

Her daughters lived extraordinary lives in the world of man, and they wore a small symbol of their ancestry inked on their left wrists. Coira knew she must wait, centuries if necessary, for the circle to come around once again and the ancient line of hags to bring the certainty of completion. So she taught her half-man, half-hag daughters how to call the wind and what herbs to mix to heal fever and the songs to calm the fussiest baby. She taught them how to summon the rain and how to listen to the hum of the ley lines that connected the earth. Then she sent them back across the Lethe into a new world that had lost its ability to believe in magic, and she waited. One day, a daughter of hers would remember, and the circle would once again be complete. Until then, the ley lines buzzed with anticipation, and the intersecting jagged lines of Ingwaz hummed with the certainty of a conclusion.

EPILOGUE

"IT'S A REAL SHAME," the woman said to no one in particular as she stood with her neighbors and surveyed what remained of the great manor house on Cathedral Court.

"The little girl, too," another woman tutted behind her.

No evidence of the remains of the little family that had moved into the manor house just a year or so past was ever found. The official word was that the fire from the lightning strike had consumed the remains, or maybe it was animals that came up from the vast stretch of land that lay beyond the manor house. The storm had been sudden and isolated to this little corner of Glasgow. The manor house had taken the lion's share of the damage, and a stray strike of lightning had burned half the grand structure.

"They worked so hard to make it nice again. Such a nice family," the neighbors murmured and then shuffled away. Truth was, the family that had lived in the now-ruined house had been a bit off-putting. "Especially the little girl, poor thing," they all whispered in the days to come. "Her father just gone and obviously a wreck. Never heard her say a word." The stories of Moira Blair and her daughter swirled once again, and eventually the passersby agreed that it was a relief when the remains of the structure were torn down for good.

The lot sat empty but for the little stone cottage at the back of the land. Many a developer drew up plans; a great line of flats, an office building, a grand hotel, even a museum was considered in the line of ideas that came and went as soon as they attempted to break ground. The great bulldozers shut down and turned on their sides in the night. The rain would break and pour down, seemingly just on the lot on Cathedral Court. The neighbors would exchange glances and pull their shades shut. Eventually, the land was left for green space and signed over to the nature conservancy instead. The grass grew high and wildflowers bloomed. Willow and rowan trees dotted the land, and children played in the shade and beauty. The stone cottage still stood, abandoned and untouched. The children would make a grand game of daring each other to sneak through the woods at the back of the land to peek in the window. It was said that on the first night of summer, the shortest night of the year, the light of a single candle could be seen flickering in the window.

The whole of Glasgow found an uncommon peace and calm in the time following the great summer storm that destroyed the manor house on Cathedral Court. It was as though the animosity and ugliness that ruled so much of the world had been lifted. Matters that would have erupted in violence and anger before seemed to melt away, and everyone said it was a lovely time and weren't we lucky to live in such a grand place? It was short-lived, however, as the women and men of Glasgow forgot what it felt to be grateful for the reprieve from the drama of the world. They crossed a Lethe of their own, and soon the world was as it had been, and the outside distraction of anger and fear and war breached the newly washed shores of Glasgow once again. But the stories still survived, and the old ones in the town talked about a line of hags who had once walked their streets—extraordinary women who in the course of telling and retelling the history had been elevated to the status of the Goddess herself. Women who could summon the winds and who knew songs to calm the fussiest baby.

Far off in her cave in the lowland crags, the Cailleach inked the symbol of the intersecting lines of Ingwaz onto her daughter's wrist. She would leave this place and forget what she had learned. But one day, perhaps, a flash of light or a bit of a song or the sound of the sea at night would spark a memory, and the circle would begin again.

ACKNOWLEDGMENTS

THANK YOU TO MY husband for listening to every idea, frustration, and inspiration and for talking me out of a thousand trees. Thank you to my son for being a constant reminder of what is important, and for keeping me sane with your overall awesomeness.

Thank you to Todd Bottorff and Turner Publishing Group for this opportunity. Independent publishers are the heart and soul of the book universe, and I am forever grateful for your belief in my work. Thank you to Stephanie Bowman, Jon O'Neal, Leslie Hinson, Stephen Turner, Madeline Cothren, and everyone else at Turner who worked on this project.

I come from an extraordinary line of women. They are smart, strong, and have never been known to suffer a fool. While *Hag* is, overall, a work of fiction, my mother filled my childhood with stories about her life and the history of my grandmother and great-grandmothers. I hope I did them proud, and I hope they forgive the creative liberties that come with storytelling.

I binge-listened to Kate Rusby, Sarah Jarosz, and Stevie Nicks while writing *Hag*. Thank you for the inspiration and clarity.

And thank you to beautiful Ciel, whose cabin in the woods provided not only a perfect writer's retreat but vision on how to live a more connected life.